THE HAUNTING OF BOB CRATCHIT

INSPIRED BY
CHARLES DICKENS' A CHRISTMAS CAROL

BY
BRENDON MAROTTA &
DAVID JOHN MAROTTA

Brendon Marotta & David John Marotta
1000 Ednam Center, Suite 300,
Charlottesville, VA 22903
(434) 244-0000

The Haunting of Bob Cratchit / Brendon Marotta & David John Marotta
1st ed. Rev. 20.

Hardcover: 978-1-7362723-0-5
Paperback: 978-1-7362723-1-2
eBook: 978-1-7362723-2-9

CONTENTS

STAVE ONE

TINY TIM WAS SICK to begin with. There is no doubt whatever about that. The signs of ill health were present in his cough, his crutch, his unsteady gait, and most evidently the unnaturally shrunken stature of his six-year-old physique. His father knew it, and no one cared for Tim more than Bob Cratchit. Tim was as sick as a dog.

Mind! I must confess that I have known many a mutt in my day that was more discernably healthy than poor Tiny Tim. Indeed, I have never been inclined myself to regard the dog as a categorically unwell species of animal. But the wisdom of our ancestors is in the simile, and my unhallowed hands shall not disturb it, or the Country's done for. You will therefore permit me to repeat emphatically that Tiny Tim was as sick as a dog.

Did Bob fear for Tiny Tim's life? Of course he did. How could it be otherwise? In the span of one short year, Bob had seen his son's health deteriorate from that of a normal boy to the unfortunate circumstances of his present state. To this, Bob had been his son's primary witness, his most involved spectator, his most optimistic observer, his most ardent encourager, and his stalwart pillar of support. And through it all, even Bob had retreated and welcomed habits that obscured those more terrible implications of Tim's ever-worsening condition.

The mention of Tim's condition brings me back to the point I started from. There is no doubt that Tiny Tim was sick. This much was immediately obvious. It was plain for all to see in the boy's frail form—a frailness that couldn't be disguised no matter how many layers of clothing were bundled over his meek little frame. Today, the number of layers was five. Five layers of tattered, threadbare, second-hand garments, and Tiny Tim was grateful for each one.

Like many days, today found Tim perched atop a pew in the great London cathedral with his legs dangling off the seat, child-sized crutch propped up beside him. His blond head was bowed, his blue eyes were shut, and his mittened hands were clasped together in prayer.

It was the morning of Christmas Eve, and the cathedral was vast, vibrant, and cold—as cold as the rest of London on that merciless winter day. The towering curtains of stone that made up the structure's walls might as well have been sheets of glacial ice, and the many painted tiles that made up the floor might as well have been the face of a frozen over lake. A great number of candles in polished brass stands did their part to light the holy place with all due holiday cheer, but they were powerless to fend off the chill. It was here in this candlelit chasm of stone where Tiny Tim could be found: a lone little bundle of warmth in the otherwise vacant cathedral's freezing abyss.

Tim was praying with great vigor today, and his prayers were visibly slipping from his mouth in puffs of condensation. His head was bowed towards an immaculate stained glass window that loomed above his pew. It depicted

Christ the babe in the manger, awe-stricken animals and gift-laden wise men gathered around him in reverence. The scene's red, blue, green, and golden panes were all aglow from the sun as it climbed the eastern sky outside.

"Dear Lord," whispered Tim, "I pray that this Christmas you send your Holy Spirits. . ."

The lad's lisp had put a plural on the word, turning "Spirit" into "Spirits." It was a detail that did not go unnoticed by the good Lord above.

". . . to be with my father, and with Mister Scrooge, and with everyone we know. Please make us grateful, and teach us the true meaning of Christmas. And may God bless us, each and every one. Amen."

The final word passed through his lips in a soft cloud of mist and, as it did, a curtain of mist likewise descended on the grounds of the cathedral at large. The mist thickened into fog as it crept in all directions. It overtook the old parish cemetery that bordered the cathedral, swallowing up row after row of crumbling headstones like a spectral wave rolling in over the shore. When there were no rows of headstones left to swallow, the ghostly shroud overflowed the sacred grounds of the dead, spilling into the city of London. By mid-morning, the fog would blanket the entire city, washing out the sun and obscuring every court and lane and crooked little side-street.

Back in the cemetery, the tendrils of fog were curling 'round one grave marker in particular. From a source unseen, an unnatural gust of wind sprung to life amid the blurry silhouettes of mist-laden headstones. As if directed by a hidden hand, the gust hurtled through the graveyard along a deliberate path towards this chosen stone, eerie trails of displaced vapor twisting in its wake. It came to a halt when it reached the headstone, which bore the following name: JACOB MARLEY.

The date engraved beneath the name marked the grave's occupant as seven years deceased to the day. The wind roared over the headstone, and something from beyond the veil emerged to meet its call. Although there were no eyes to see it, the shadow of a phantom passed over the grave. Although there were no ears to hear it, the rattle of a chain echoed throughout the yard.

Little did Tiny Tim know he had set in motion the events of that famous Christmas. You may have heard the story of Ebenezer Scrooge and his Christmas Carol, but few know the story of his lowly clerk, a story that began the very same night . . . the story of the haunting of Bob Cratchit.

In a dreary but esteemed place of business a few blocks away from the cathedral, Tiny Tim's father, Bob Cratchit, sat hunched over a desk that was covered in unsorted documents, pen in hand, scratching away at a letter. He was a middle-aged man and always wore a patched and threadbare suit that was a size too large for his skinny physique. His skin was pale, his eyes were blue, and his hair was thick and dark.

The side office in which Bob spent the majority of his workweek was only as wide as the empty door frame that made up the entrance to the room. Inside, there was just enough floorspace to accommodate a wobbly desk, hard wood stool, and small fireplace for warmth on harsh winter days such as these. One wall of the work nook was actually the building's storefront window with the words SCROOGE AND MARLEY painted across the glass in faded letters.

Opposite that, a thin wall with a built-in glass divider separated the nook from the building's main interior. It was in this much more spacious area where Bob's employer—Ebenezer Scrooge—helmed the business from his quite comfortable seat at his completely stable desk.

Presently, however, Scrooge had redirected his chilling presence to the doorframe of Bob's office. He was a hollow-cheeked, thin-lipped old man with coarse white hair, bushy eyebrows, and bristling sideburns. Still more wiry hair clung to his sharply jutting chin. His nose was long and pointed. His tailored suit was of a plain design but made from high-quality material, and within its creaseless fabric, he carried himself with the most rigid of postures.

"Do you have the investment package?" Scrooge demanded, hand outstretched. His voice had a sharp, grating timbre at the best of times, but it sounded even harsher than usual today.

"Right here, sir," answered Bob, quickly finding a folder from the stack of papers on his desk and handing it up to his employer. Scrooge gave it a stern look over then said to Bob's immense surprise, "I've never seen anyone run the numbers so quickly . . ."

"Thank you, sir," said Bob, brightening at the compliment.

". . . and forget to insure it," finished Scrooge with a withering glare.

Bob recoiled. "It's not my fault, Mister Scrooge!" he protested. "Marley was always the one who purchased insurance."

"Marley's not here anymore, is he?" shot back Scrooge. He jabbed a gnarled finger towards the faded storefront lettering on the window beside them—SCROOGE AND MARLEY. Scrooge had never bothered to have the sign repainted since Marley's death, deeming it a superfluous expense.

"No, sir," Bob sighed in response.

"Have you even written the investors and collected their stake?" asked Scrooge.

Bob pushed the ledger he'd been working on aside to scramble through the papers on his desk.

"What are their names again?" he asked.

Scrooge clenched his jaw. "You need to know this, Bob."

Bob located the list of names Scrooge was looking for. He handed the paper to Scrooge and, joking, said, "Good thing our business has you, sir, to be the one who's good with people."

Scrooge answered the remark with a blank, unflinching stare. A tense silence descended on the office as the coldness of Scrooge's gaze grew more frigid than ever.

"Need I remind you, Mister Cratchit, that I'm not the one who needs this money."

Bob shifted about on his stool as he fought hard to keep the joking smile on his face from giving way.

"If you'd like, sir, I could pay you to work here," replied Bob.

Scrooge's stony expression remained unchanged in the face of Bob's attempt at humor. The tense silence returned and lingered on for an uncomfortable series of moments. Then Scrooge cut through the quiet all at once with one of his infamous tirades.

"If I fire you and refuse to give you a reference, you'll never find work again. You won't even be able to start your own business. You and your family will starve. Is that what you want?"

Bob felt the color draining from his cheeks. He looked down to fidget with his hands in his lap while Scrooge turned his gaze back to the ledger, leaving Bob to squirm in anxious quiet for some time. When the inspection was finally complete, Scrooge said stiffly, "It is good work."

"Thank you, sir," breathed Bob, the tension in his body going slack.

"How can you be so good at your job," Scrooge asked, "yet not dependable?'

The question put a sour taste in the back of Bob's throat as he searched for a reply. While he racked his brain, images of days gone by when Marley still lived rose to the surface of his mind's eye. Instead of Scrooge peering down his beak at the ledger, Bob saw Marley checking over the work as he had done: line by line, a lively nod for every record that read clean, a quick, careless wobble of the head for every fault, quickly followed by a brief but impassioned lesson as to how Bob could avoid the error in the future. Marley, Bob was sure, would have met Bob's lapse in memory with some sort of lesson about writing down important tasks in short-hand on a scrap of paper to be kept in prominent view. Where Scrooge's criticism was scathing, Marley's had always been constructive.

Amidst this unexpected flood of memories, the only answer Bob could find to offer Scrooge came out of his mouth in a mutter.

"It's not my fault, sir."

Scrooge scowled. "Write the investors," he ordered, tossing the list back on top of a pile of papers on Bob's desk. Shaking his head, he turned and left the office.

In the wake of Scrooge's wrath, Bob looked down to find that his hands were ever so slightly atremble. He flexed and stretched his fingers, hoping to shake off the quiver—but to no avail. The shaking continued.

Despite his mounting tremors, Bob set his mind back on the task at hand as best he could. As the hours drifted by, however, the trembling grew worse. Just as he was putting the final touches on a shipping manifest he'd spent a large part of the afternoon transcribing, the trembling rose into a quake he could scarcely contain. The quivering was so severe that Bob's hand blotted ink all down the page, ruining the document and undoing all his work. Bob cursed under his breath.

At that, an image of the tavern Bob often frequented after work sprang to life in his mind's eye: fire roaring cozily in the hearth, a tankard of ale in his hand. What Bob wouldn't give for a good swig of such a drink right now.

As if on cue, a booming voice from outside on the street could be heard yelling, "Christmas special! A free bag of chestnuts for every half pint of gin!"

Peering through the storefront window—and through the thick curtain of fog that had seized the city since that morning—Bob saw the owner of the voice wheeling a gin cart down the court. As he watched, a gaggle of children appeared out of the fog and swarmed the cart like merry fleas to a mutt, only for the merchant to swat them away. When they were gone, the cart owner bellowed his special Christmas offer again.

"Christmas special! A free bag of chestnuts for every half pint of gin!"

Bob licked his lips. He looked down at his trembling hand then up towards the clock that hung over the fireplace. It was almost five. Bob resolved that he could make it through the rest of his shift without the aid of the gin. He could wait.

Bob picked up his pen. When he put it to work against a fresh sheet of paper, the shaking in his hand returned, worse than ever. It rendered his writing entirely illegible. Ugly blots of ink pooled up on the page. Bob balled up the sheet of paper and hurled it into the fireplace. He swore again under his breath, then looked back to the street where the gin merchant was still meandering about. Bob checked in on Scrooge through the divider to find him well-occupied at his desk. Was it possible that Bob could slip away for a drink and return before his absence was noticed?

The ever-searching, ever-scrutinizing eye of Scrooge must have noticed Bob looking about, for now he was squawking:

"Not one more piece of coal. I don't care how cold you are."

Bob looked over at Scrooge through the divider to find the man fixing him with a glare and curled lip.

"Yes," offered Bob, shifting uneasily in his seat, "that's it. I'm just shivering."

"Don't you have a coat?" probed Scrooge.

"I can't afford one," Bob returned.

"You only need to buy a coat once," chided Scrooge. "You have to buy coal every time you use it."

Bob settled himself on his stool, resigned to Scrooge's logic. The thought of slipping outside to purchase the half-pint was discarded. In truth, Bob had a life or death request that he planned to make of Scrooge before the day was done, and he knew that whatever meager portion of mercy the man possessed could only be spread so thin.

A tinkling of the bell above the business's door announced the arrival of a visitor. Looking up through the door frame of his office to the building's front threshold, Bob saw the finely clothed figure of Scrooge's nephew, Fred, bound into the shop. He was a slender, sharp-featured man. His face–ruddy and handsome–was especially lively today as he strode with open arms towards Scrooge, cheeks flushed red with good cheer.

"A merry Christmas, uncle! God save you!" Fred roared.

"Bah! Humbug!" Scrooge spat back.

"Christmas a humbug, uncle? You don't mean that, I'm sure."

"I do," Scrooge affirmed as he swept his stony gaze over Fred. Bob recognized the look. It was the same way Scrooge raked his eyes over Bob's work–disapprovingly.

"Merry Christmas!" Scrooge went on, spitefully. "What right have you to be merry? What reason have you to be merry? You're poor enough."

"What right have you to be dismal?" retorted Fred. "What reason have you to be morose? You're rich enough."

"Bah! Humbug!"

Watching the scene unfold from behind the glass divider of his nook, Bob licked his lips a second time. Seeing Fred's unflinching merriment was triggering Bob's craving for a drink once again. As Scrooge launched into a tirade on the fallacies of Christmas, Bob slid open the bottommost drawer of his desk and reached a shaky hand inside, fishing around in the abyss until his trembling fingers closed around the familiar shape of a bottle.

"What else can I be when I live in such a world of fools as this?" Scrooge was raging. "Merry Christmas! Out upon merry Christmas. What's Christmas time to you but . . ."

Keeping one eye on Scrooge to make sure he wasn't caught, Bob plucked the bottle from the drawer and stole a glance at its contents. A small swig's worth of whiskey was still puddled at the bottom.

". . . a time for paying bills without money; a time for finding yourself a year older, but not an hour richer; a time for balancing your books and having every item in 'em through a round dozen of months presented against you?"

Bob gulped down the whiskey with one fluid motion. Then he returned the bottle to the drawer, slid it shut, and wiped his mouth with the back of his hand. The hand was steady now. Just like that, the drink had done the trick.

Back in action at last, Bob tuned out Scrooge's ranting and got back to work. Soon he was tearing through the pile of unfinished letters on his desk at full speed. A stack of sealed and ready envelopes began to grow beside him at a rapid rate. Bob was only roused from his concentrated effort when his boss's voice grew too fierce to ignore.

"Good afternoon," Bob heard him snap.

"I'll keep my Christmas humor to the last," returned Fred. "So, a Merry Christmas, uncle!"

"Good afternoon."

"And a happy New Year!"

"Good afternoon!"

Bob heard footsteps on their way from Scrooge's desk and looked up just in time to catch Fred's eye as he was reaching for the door to leave the premise. Fred grinned.

"Merry Christmas, Mister Cratchit."

Once more, Bob cast a cautious eye around his surroundings—this time to ensure Scrooge wouldn't overhear Bob utter the forbidden words: "Merry Christmas to you too, sir," in cheerful reply. Then he drew himself to his feet to see Fred, whom Bob had always counted as a friend, out the door.

"There's another fellow, my clerk," came Scrooge's grating voice, "with fifteen shillings a week, and a wife and family, talking about a merry Christmas. I'll retire to Bedlam."

No sooner had Bob seen Fred out than more visitors arrived to replace him. This time, two well-dressed, portly gentlemen had stepped into the building off the street. The pair of jolly strangers smiled and bowed towards Bob in greeting as they swept their hats off their heads.

"Have I the pleasure of addressing Mister Scrooge, or Mister Marley?" asked one.

"Mister Marley has been dead these seven years," barked Scrooge from his desk. "He died seven years ago, this very night." With a stiff wave, he beckoned the gentlemen to approach him. They bustled past Bob towards Scrooge.

When they'd reached his desk, one of the gentlemen remarked, "We have no doubt that Mister Marley's liberality–"

Scrooge's body gave a visible shudder at the word.

"–is well represented by his surviving partner." The man produced a card from the inside of his overcoat and handed it to Scrooge. Scrooge frowned, shook his head, and handed it back without so much as a glance.

"At this festive season of the year, Mister Scrooge," the other gentleman pressed, "it is more than usually desirable that we should make some slight provision for the poor and destitute, who suffer greatly at the present time."

"Are there no prisons?" asked Scrooge.

At that, Bob shook his head and, having heard enough, turned and set off from the door frame of the building's entrance towards his office. As he did, Bob saw something that froze him in his tracks and made the hairs on the back of his neck stand up on end.

Framed like a portrait by the door frame to Bob's office was none other than Marley, seated at Bob's desk, looking just as Bob remembered him. Only now, his expression was blank, his eyes wide and unblinking.

"Marley?" breathed Bob, unable to say the name any louder than a whisper with his throat tightened up in terror. He had believed the man long dead!

Bob felt a hand grab his shoulder from behind. At once he whirled around—nearly jumping out of his skin—to find Fred holding a fresh bottle of gin from the cart. Somehow, he'd slipped back inside without Bob's notice. The yelp of fear that had been building in Bob's chest slipped through his lips as a silent exhale.

"You look like you've seen a ghost," Fred observed.

Bob looked back to his desk. It was empty. Of course it was empty. Marley hadn't been sitting there. The prospect of having to ask Scrooge for help with Tiny Tim's medicine was weighing Bob's mind down into madness. That was all.

"Here," said Fred, holding out the bottle of gin. "Have a drink."

Bob gladly took him up on the offer. He accepted the bottle, took a generous swig, and handed it back.

"Thank you," said Bob. "Perhaps this will give me the courage to ask Scrooge if he can help my son . . ."

Fred was midway through a sip of gin as Bob confessed his intent to beg for Scrooge's financial assistance in the matter of Tiny Tim's declining health. Fred nearly choked and spat out his drink at the premise.

"Courage?!" he exclaimed. "That's a fool's errand."

"Yes," admitted Bob, "but . . ." Bob's voice trailed away, unable to bring life to the dreaded words. "Tim could die."

The idea frightened him more than the ghastly apparition he thought his tired, muddled mind had just tricked him into seeing.

"Bob, as your friend," said Fred, "I suggest you don't do it. I can't even get him to say yes to Christmas dinner."

"My son is very ill," Bob explained. It was as close an approximation to the grim reality of the situation as he could bear to speak aloud. His voice had quaked as he said it.

"I'm so sorry," offered Fred, reaching out and clasping Bob's shoulder. "It would be a great blessing if he even gave you a day off."

Bob nodded.

They drank until they reached the bottom of the bottle. Fred handed it to Bob for him to have the last swig.

"Merry Christmas, Bob," said Fred. And with that, he took his leave from the premise for good.

Bob made the short trek back to his work cell to the sound of heated discussion coming from Scrooge's desk.

"Many can't go there; and many would rather die," one of the portly gentlemen was saying.

"If they would rather die," Scrooge returned, "they had better do it, and decrease the surplus population. Good afternoon, gentleman!"

The gentlemen exchanged a glance with one another. A moment later, they were marching back towards the building's entrance, hats in hand. Bob offered them a sympathetic look as they passed by the doorway to his office, which they met with a nod. They left, and Bob returned to his work.

The return was short-lived, because soon the clock was chiming six, signaling the end of Bob's workday. The street outside had gone dark now, and the storefront window was nearly frosted over. As Bob looked over the veins of ice that had formed in the glass, the face of a small boy appeared, pressed up against the pane and peering inside. The boy's face vanished as quickly as it had appeared, only to be replaced by the sweet sound of song drifting in from the street. A band of youthful carolers were assembled outside the shop, singing.

"God bless you, merry gentleman.

May nothing you dismay!

Remember Christ our savior

Was born on Christmas Day."

Scrooge sped past Bob's office and flung the front door open, brandishing his favorite ruler like an officer's baton.

"To save us all from"–

The sweet-sounding melody transformed into a cacophony of panic as Scrooge burst forth from the business, waving the piece of wood at the carolers and snarling. The children scattered, all save one–a less attentive lad left alone singing:

"Satan's"–

Thankfully, his wits caught up with the threat of Scrooge looming over him on the building's front step, poised to lash out with his switch. The boy then turned and joined his friends in retreat, only to crash head first into the gin cart that was parked in the night's abyss just a few feet away.

"Bah!" Scrooge huffed. He turned back inside and threw the door shut behind him.

Bob gathered his things to leave as slowly as he could, giving his employer's temper some time to settle down. When he could stall his departure no longer, Bob approached Scrooge to be dismissed for the night and prepared to ask him for his charity in the matter of Tiny Tim's medicine.

"You'll want all day tomorrow, I suppose," Scrooge scoffed as he approached.

"If quite convenient, sir," answered Bob.

"It's not convenient, and it's not fair. If I was to dock your pay half a crown for it, you'd think yourself ill-used."

"And yet," Scrooge continued, "you don't think me ill-used when I pay a day's wages for no work." Scrooge rose from his seat and began to collect his possessions.

"It's only once a year," Bob protested as politely as he could.

"A poor excuse for picking a man's pocket every twenty-fifth of December!" Scrooge spat.

As they spoke, Scrooge fastened his coat up to his chin with violent twisting motions, as though every button had done him great harm.

"But I suppose," he went on, "you must have the whole day. Be here all the earlier in the morning."

Bob nodded stiffly. Then, he opened his mouth to speak. Despite Fred's warning—despite Bob's own better instinct—he was about to throw caution to the wind and ask for Scrooge's help.

Before he could loosen the words from his tongue, Scrooge shot him a withering glare that caused Bob's courage to collapse. His mouth closed. His lips sealed shut. He said nothing.

Scrooge walked away, grumbling under his breath, and Bob took his leave.

Bob pulled his over-sized suit jacket around him for warmth as he stepped outside. Looking ahead down the narrow, dimly lit court, he saw the two portly gentlemen exiting a neighboring business. Bob quickened his pace to catch up with them.

"Oh, excuse me—" Bob began, coming up on their heels, but one of the men cut him off, calling back, "Don't worry sir, we shan't be bothering your office anymore." Neither of the gentlemen seemed interested in stopping to chat. Not wanting them to get the wrong idea of him, Bob called after the two men.

"Oh no, I'm not like Mister Scrooge sir. I support your work."

That stopped the gentleman in their tracks. In unison, they halted, turned, and extended their full attention to Bob.

"That's wonderful!" said one. "We appreciate your support."

"Yes, just wonderful," echoed the other. "How much should we put you down for?"

"What?" asked Bob, a frown forming on his lips.

"How much would you like to contribute?"

"Oh," said Bob, shaking his head, "nothing for me."

The gentlemen exchanged a narrow-eyed look with one another.

"But Mister Scrooge," Bob piped up, "he should have supported you."

"He did not support us at all," nodded the second of the men.

"Exactly," said Bob.

The gentlemen exchanged another look. The first had cocked an eyebrow. The second's lips were pursed.

"And you want to support us for . . ." the first gentleman began.

"–Oh, I would like to support you for a handsome sum," finished Bob, eagerly.

"Capital!" exclaimed the man. "How much?"

"Well," chortled Bob, "if it were up to me, I'd give you all his profits for a week!"

"Whose profits?"

"Mister Scrooge's," answered Bob.

"Wouldn't that be embezzlement?" asked the second gentleman.

"We wouldn't want you to do anything illegal," added the first.

"Oh, I don't mean to actually give you his profits," explained Bob.

Now the men's eyes were beginning to bulge out of their heads in blatant frustration.

"How exactly do you propose we feed anyone without donations?" demanded one.

"You know we're actually trying to feed people," snapped the other.

"Of course," Bob explained, "I'm very much in favor of the whole idea."

The first of the two gentlemen spoke, the harsh edge of anger in his voice unconcealed.

"Is there some amount of provision which you would like to make for those less fortunate than yourself–"

"–from your own earnings!" interjected the second gentleman.

"From your own earnings," echoed his partner, "or are you only generous with other people's money?"

Bob looked back and forth between the men, blinking. "Well, I need my money," he tried to explain. "I have to pay off the Christmas goose."

"And where exactly are you getting that?" asked the second gentleman.

"The Camden Tavern!" Bob exclaimed. "It's the best deal in London."

The gentlemen exchanged a final look. This time, their expressions were blank. A gust of wind swept over the street as the pair of them stood there in silence.

"Would you like to come with me?" offered Bob.

They didn't. And so, Bob walked the short trek to the tavern without the portly gentlemen.

Camden Town's tavern was a lesser known establishment tucked away in an alley midway between Scrooge's place of business and the great London cathedral. Outside, the windowpanes were cracked, and the door hung crooked in its frame. Inside, a fine mixture of sawdust and rat droppings layered the floor while the smog of a chimney in dire need of sweeping choked the air. The tables and chairs were all battered to oblivion, as though they'd all seen the bad end of one too many drunken bar fights over the years, and much the same could be said of the regulars who frequented the pub. To the vast majority of those who knew about the tavern, it was a seedy and undesirable place to be. To Bob, it was a comfortable venue in which to unwind.

"What'll it be, Bob?" asked the barkeep. He was an older chap who always wore an apron with so many stains that its original color had long become indiscernible, and under that lay his worn and tattered sailor's uniform from his days in the service. His skin was taut and leathery, his brawny jaw unshaven, and his demeanor all around less-than-jovial.

"The usual," answered Bob.

"It's two drinks if you want to pay off tomorrow's goose," the barkeep reminded him. Like most bars, Camden Town's tavern had one of the few public ovens. And they had a deal where you received a free Christmas goose with enough drinks.

"Then the usual," replied Bob. "Twice."

"That's the Christmas spirit," said the barkeep, fetching him a cup. He started to pour. "You won't find a better deal in London. A free goose every Christmas for any patron who orders fifty drinks between All Saints Day and Christmas."

He finished pouring and slid the first drink across the counter to Bob.

Bob took his first sip of the night since getting off work. The setting of the tavern might have left something to be desired, but the drinks never failed to appease Bob's desire for intoxication. It was said that the barkeep's brewer aimed to numb the patron's palette before they could be turned away by the taste.

The taste had never bothered Bob. He took another long draw from his cup.

"By the way," said the barkeep, "did you hear? Fagin passed. Hanged. By all accounts, he deserved it too." The barkeep had Bob's second drink pressed against his palm, already poured. He slid it down the bar with a nudge, where it came to rest next to Bob's first, already half empty mug.

"I'd have never found this place without him," said Bob, taking the drink. "We should toast him. It's Christmas after all. Everyone deserves a toast."

The bartender shook his grizzly head. "I won't waste a whole drink on a thief."

"Then a toast to the dead," Bob compromised. "To all those who have moved on from this life to the next."

With a shrug and a nod, the barkeep poured himself a drink. "To the dead."

Both men raised their cups, and Bob made a toast.

"May the wisdom gained from those who have gone before us guide us in our pilgrimage on earth. May they one day rise again in the hope of the resurrection of our Lord and Saviour born this Christmas day."

The barkeep gave a half-hearted shrug. Then, they tapped their cups together and drank. As they did, the clamor of the raucous tavern goers in the background seemed to grow dim. When Bob brought the cup back down on the bar, he heard it land not with the thud of wood hitting wood, but with the distinct rattle of chains.

Bob blinked, decided that he must be hearing things, and reached for his second drink. The moment his fingers brushed the rim of the cup laid out before him, a cold and terrible sensation crept up his arm as though the blood coursing through his veins had turned into ice. Bob yanked back his hand and looked at the cup with wide, unblinking eyes. As he looked, a coat of frost crackled up the cup's side. Then the rattling sound filled Bob's ears again.

Bob twisted his head left and right and found, to his terror and amazement, that the tavern was empty.

The rattling sound drew closer. Bob could hear it coming directly from behind him where he sat at the bar. Slowly, not wanting to do it but unable to resist, Bob turned himself around in his stool.

Sure enough, the rattling sound was coming from a chain being dragged across the floor. It belonged to none other than Jacob Marley, seven years deceased to the day. The chain was clasped around the middle of his coat, and from there it wound around him and behind him like a grim metal tail made up of cash-boxes, keys, padlocks, ledgers, deeds, and heavy purses wrought in steel. Marley himself was ghastly white with a tourniquet tied around his head from the bottom of his chin to the top of his skull. As Bob watched, Marley unfastened the tourniquet and his pale jaw fell open, limp as a dead fish. The shade let out a low moan, then said:

"I see you got one for me."

Marley reached out and took the frost-covered cup off the bar.

"Marley . . ." was all Bob could say.

Marley smiled, held up the drink, and tipped it cheekily towards Bob in mocking toast.

"To the dead," Marley said. Then he downed the rum, and Bob's insides squirmed in protest as he watched the amber liquid pass through the phantom's lips. It trickled down through Marley's translucent body and splashed onto the floor.

" . . . I thought you were dead," whimpered Bob.

"I am." He handed the empty cup back to Bob. Bob took it. It was freezing.

"Why–why are you here?" Bob stammered.

"I've come from your employer," answered the shade.

"Ebenezer Scrooge is my employer," asserted Bob.

"He who sent me would disagree."

Bob ran a hand back through his hair. It was wet with cold sweat.

"Marley, is that really you?" Bob asked.

"It is what I've become," answered the shade.

"There isn't much left of you," Bob remarked.

"There isn't much left of you, either," shot back Marley. "I'm here to talk about what you have become."

Bob bored his eyes into the cup, hoping he would find something in its contents to explain this impossible event. "Someone who sees things when he drinks?" he offered up, half-joking, half-worried the joke was a mere statement of fact.

Marley let out a wail. "Ohhh!" he moaned, chain rattling. "Why will no mortals believe in the spiritual world even when it breaks through and is finally visible to their senses! I am the one who is seeing things, and what I've seen is driving me senseless."

"You are particular for a hallucination," said Bob.

Marley raised a frightful cry, shaking his chain all the harder and wailing with redoubled misery. His wailing shook the foundation until every pane of window glass in the place was rattling alongside his chain. The door flung open and an icy gust of winter air blew in from outside. The gust snuffed out the hearth, whisked the flame off every wick, and brought the tavern to the brink of total darkness.

Bob fell to his knees before Marley's ghost.

"Mercy!" he cried. "Dreadful apparition, why do you trouble me?"

"Man of the worldly mind," Marley said, "do you believe me or not?"

"Yes—yes, I do," answered Bob. "But why do you come to me only now after I have been drinking?"

The apparition rolled his eyes. "On what days do you not stop for a drink?"

Bob mulled over the phantom's words.

"I see your point," he conceded. "But why haunt me at all?"

"I am doomed to wander through the world and witness what I cannot share but might have shared had my time been better employed," Marley shook his chain with both hands. Its coils writhed like angry snakes. "Woe is me!"

"You're really depressing," Bob said.

"I'm dead," Marley flatly replied.

"You are bound as well," Bob noted.

"Every link in this chain was forged from the choices I made. From my fear, my greed, my pride. Instead of grateful arms to bear me up, I have all the selfish cares of life weighing me down."

With that, he snatched the cup from Bob's hand once again and turned towards the bar, elating Bob at the prospect of a refill. The shade proceeded to pass through the bar and put the cup away.

"Each man's pattern is different," Marley said as he drifted back through the solid wood that made up the bar. "Is mine so strange to you? Perhaps your own would be more familiar."

"Mine?" said Bob, tilting his head to the side. "I have no riches that weigh me down."

"Lacking riches does not mean we value the right things, nor that we do not covet the riches of others," replied the shade.

"Have you no good news for me?" asked Bob outright.

"Good news comes from the other realm and is conveyed by ministers even less welcome than I. I cannot tell you all I would. Nor can I linger. Heed what you can receive. I'm driven tonight and must warn others as well."

"I need no warning, ghost of Mister Marley," Bob assured him. "I'm right as rain. And I have all day off tomorrow for celebrating."

"What good is resting the seventh day if you have failed in your labor the other six?"

Bob frowned. Marley turned to pace about the room, chains rattling, cash-boxes and other burdens scraping over floorboards in his wake.

"Ages of incessant labor by immortal creatures will be required before the good of this world will be fully developed. And every Christian spirit working kindly in its little sphere, whatever it may be, will find its mortal life too short for its full means of usefulness!"

Marley ceased his pacing and looked at Bob directly. "And if I, who had no one depending on me, failed in my business, how much more so have you?"

"But I'm not in business, Mister Marley. You and Scrooge are the ones in business."

"You are your business. Your family is your business. Your labor is your business. Did he who came to redeem the world leave you unchanged?"

"If only you could see how hard I've worked, Mister Marley," pleaded Bob. The ghost scowled, took a seat next to him at the bar, and fixed him with a penetrating stare.

"For seven years, I have sat invisible beside you. How it is you can see me now I cannot tell, but tonight I am here to warn you."

"But I don't understand what peril I'm in," protested Bob.

"No! You don't understand! Your position, your family, your marriage, and even the very life of your youngest son–"

To this, Bob's stomach gave a lurch. His shoulders caved inward.

"–depends upon this failure to understand, and that is why you will be haunted by three spirits."

"Haunted by three spirits?" repeated Bob.

"Without their visits, you cannot hope to turn from the path you are on. The first will visit this very night as the clock strikes one. Expect the second on Christmas day. And the third tomorrow when the last stroke of twelve has ceased to vibrate."

"Couldn't we do it all in one night?" urged Bob, perking up slightly from his slump.

Marley's ghost shook his head and let out a sigh. With a tone of finality in his voice, he replied, "You are not the only one the spirits are visiting tonight."

Marley rose off his barstool and drifted back towards the entrance to the tavern.

"You will see more, but remember what has passed between us!" he cried. As he spoke, he withdrew the tourniquet he'd been wearing from the ruffled fringes of his coat and wrapped it back around his head. When he pulled it tight, his jaw snapped into place against the rest of his skull with a nauseating crack that made Bob flinch.

The shade walked backwards out the open door. The wailing of self-accusatory spirits echoed as he faded into the snowstorm behind him. The door closed. The sound of the bar returned to normal. Bob turned back to the bar and looked down at his drink. A voice in his ear sent a jolt of surprise through his body.

"Bob? Bob!" someone was saying. Bob blinked and looked up from his cup to find the barkeep eying him warily with a scowl.

"You've been staring at that drink for a quarter of an hour."

"I have?" asked Bob. He looked around. Everything was as it had been before his old boss's shade had appeared. The pub was filled with the din of drunken hollering from the other guests all around him. The hearth was roaring. The candles were burning in their stands.

"Pull it together," the barkeep barked. "Your kid is here to see you."

"Hello, Father!" piped up a squeaky voice that Bob knew very well.

Bob looked down to find Tiny Tim's bright blue eyes smiling up at him. The boy was still bundled up in the five layers of ragged, rough-spun clothing Emily had dressed him in that morning. He was balancing on his crutch beside Bob's barstool, little body fidgeting with excitement in spite of his limited mobility.

"Have you been there this whole time?" asked Bob, his eyes going wide.

"I didn't want to disturb you while you were praying into your cup, father."

Across the counter, the barkeep let out a derisive snort.

Bob fought to quell the sensation of guilt he felt rising in his torso from showing on his face. "How did you find me here?" he asked.

"You're always here after work. Oh, Father, I love that I always know where to find you."

Bob wasn't sure if it was a compliment his son always knew to find him at the bar. He rose to his feet, stumbling a bit from the rush of blood to his skull brought on by the act. Steadying himself, he asked, "Did you walk the whole way here? Tim, let me carry you."

"I don't mind being a cripple, Father," Tim said in an upbeat tone as Bob hoisted him onto his shoulders. "It might be a pleasant reminder to those in church of the one who made lame beggars walk and blind men see."

"Where did you find him?" the barkeep said, head cocked to the side as he looked blankly at the boy, wondering what kind of child would be happy to be a cripple if it reminded others of the good Lord.

Bob ignored the remark. "C'mon Tim," he said. "Let's go home."

The two of them tottered out onto the street where, between the dark foggy night and the blur of his own inebriated vision, Bob could scarcely make out the cobblestones beneath his feet. In spite of this, he found himself inspired to take on the manner of a pony, much to the amusement of the miniature cavalier saddled on his shoulders. With much snorting and stamping of hooves on Bob's part, the father and son were off.

Bob galloped towards home, cutting through a park that lay abandoned in the still of the evening some block or two west of the tavern's side street. It seemed the fog and the dark were in a contest of concealing all the world this night, but still Bob's jaunting pace was unhindered by nature's impenetrable veil. By now, he knew this route home from the tavern so well he could walk it blindfolded—or so he thought.

A sudden jolt of surprise coursed through Bob's inebriated body as he reached a foot out in front of him. In his drunken daze, he had expected to be met with a step of level earth. Instead, his ragged boot had plunged through empty space until it met the ground's steep decline. Lost in his drunken gallop with Tim, Bob had failed to notice he'd ascended a hill in the act of crossing through the park.

For one frightful moment, Bob nearly teetered face forward down the snow-covered slope with Tim's frail body still perched about his neck. Somehow, Bob managed to balance himself, only to over-correct, feel his feet slip out from under him against the slick blanket of snow, and go flying down the slope at full speed on his bottom.

The world whisked past Bob unseen, concealed by the fog as it was. Icy air whipped against his face. Underneath its roar he heard Tim wheeeeee-ing in his ear with innocent, unafraid glee.

Bob sleigh ride by the seat of his pants came to a well-cushioned stop in a snowbank at the bottom of the mound.

Tim was still saddled safely around his neck, the pair of them unharmed. In fact, the child was so unharmed Bob felt him bouncing up and down on his shoulders with excitement.

"Do it again, father!" Tim cheered.

Bob breathed a sigh of relief and stood, shameful that his drinking had very nearly brought injury to his son. The realization was sobering.

Now, shaking himself off, he climbed the hill and did it all again—this time intentionally. Tim was giddy with delight; all the way down he clapped his hands and squealed with the vigor of a much healthier boy. Bob thought that surely the lad was none the wiser to the concerning truth—that their initial plunge down the slope had been spurred on by a drunken misstep.

The cold had sobered Bob some by the time they arrived at the threshold of the Cratchit residence.

Much like his meager side office meant cramped working quarters for himself, Bob's humble house didn't exactly offer an abundance of living space for his wife and their six children. But much unlike Bob's office, this building's hearth was never unduly denied the presence of a generous fire. Sure enough, Bob stepped inside to find the fireplace ablaze and filling the living room with flickering orange light. Belinda, his youngest daughter at six-years-old, and Peter, his eldest son at twelve, were playing a game of jacks by the fire.

"Father!" the latter greeted, smiling.

Bob unsaddled Tim from his shoulders to place him next to Peter, then leaned the boy's tiny crutch beside the fireplace in its usual spot. Tim only needed its help to get around when he was out and about. When he was home, the lad had all the help he needed from his family.

"Children," smiled Bob. "Where is your older sister?"

"Martha has to work till tomorrow," answered Peter. At 15-years-old, Martha was Bob's eldest daughter. Months ago, she secured a job at the nearby mill to bring home a wage that helped keep the family afloat. It was grueling work, and Bob hated that the prime years of her life on this earth had to be spent in such toil, but what else could be done?

"Bob?" came his wife Emily's voice from the doorway to the kitchen. Bob swept Peter up in a hug and gave Belinda's head a merry pat before leaving the room.

The kitchen fireplace and chimney were nearly as thick with the steam of boiling pots as the night outside was thick with fog. As Bob breathed in the vapors, the spirit of the holiday pleasures it foretold filled his nostrils: the sour-sweet notes of apple sauce, the savory waft of gravy, the bitter scent of turnip greens, and all of the indulgent aromas of a dinner that could only be afforded once a year.

Bob found Emily tending to the gravy in a little saucepan when he stepped into the kitchen. As soon as she looked up to find him present, she broke away from the cooking pot and rushed at him with open arms, wooden spoon still in hand. Bob embraced her. She was a comely woman with hazel eyes and thick brown hair that fell to her shoulders in curls. A light dusting of freckles adorned her high, pale-complexioned cheekbones. Though she was the same age as Bob down to the month, the trials of life had not worn away her youth as they had for her husband. Her eyes were not nearly as sunken and dark-circled as Bob's, her brow not nearly as creased.

"Did you ask him?" she inquired when they broke from their embrace. Bob pursed his lips as the memory of shying away from Scrooge at the workday's end resurfaced in his mind.

". . . Yes," Bob lied.

"And?" Her eyes were wide and bright, her eyebrows high with eager expectation.

"He said he'd think about it. Maybe later . . ."

Emily's face fell.

"Later?" she hissed, speaking in a notch above a whisper so the children wouldn't overhear her displeasure from the other room. "It can't wait till later! Tell Scrooge our son needs care now!"

"Tim is fine," Bob asserted, lowering his voice to match her volume. "He walked to church today all by himself."

"His condition is worsening," Emily protested. "The church he should really go to is Lourdes."

"The healing Cathedral in France?" Bob asked, scoffing.

"Thousands are healed there every year," she insisted, her voice rising. "Maybe Scrooge would finance a business trip there and you could take Tim."

"We need a real doctor, Emily," Bob reasoned. "One who will treat this scientifically–with leeches, for bloodletting."

"Bob, we can't afford leeches," Emily sighed.

"Well, what do you want me to do?" Bob shot back. "Feed him lime and castor oil like he's a sailor with scurvy?" Bob's voice was beginning to grow louder as well.

"Yes! Let's do that!" exclaimed Emily. "Let's do something! I am so tired of talk . . ."

"Where would we get limes?" cried Bob. "They don't even grow in England!"

"Well, maybe your shipping magnate boss could bring some back on the next venture you organize for him!"

"He won't!" cried Bob. "He won't spare a penny for anyone other than himself!"

Meanwhile, Tim, Peter, and Belinda sat on the living room floor with toys untouched in front of them, their attention held captive by the argument ensuing in the neighboring room.

Tim hung his head on his frail little shoulders as their parents' voices rose. Peter put a hand on his brother's shoulder.

"It's not your fault, Tim," he said.

Tim rubbed at his eye and said, "At least Father got his medicine today."

Peter looked away, face riddled with a half-contained scowl.

Back in the kitchen, somewhere in the midst of the argument, the two of them had worked their voices into shouts. Perhaps they'd been shouting for some time, but only now did Bob notice. He saw the realization mirrored in his wife, whose face had gone pale as her eyes darted towards the living room where Peter, Belinda, and Tim were still gathered by the hearth.

"What if you quit and started your own firm?" asked Emily, her hushed tones resumed. "You know investors."

"That wouldn't work. I'd need a reference."

"You could get a second job," she suggested, gently. "Just for the reference."

"And how would I do that?" returned Bob. "No . . . there's nothing I can do."

Bob sidled past her to reach for a cabinet. He withdrew a wooden cup and a bottle of wine. Emily frowned.

"Bob, I love you," she began, "but we have six children. Let me help you find a way." Gently, she placed a hand over his–the hand that was holding the cup.

Bob felt the warmth of her fingers clasped over his own. Her eyes were just as warm. "Sure," Bob said.

He brushed her hand away and held tight to the cup.

"But not tonight."

Bob poured himself a drink.

STAVE TWO

ONE CUP OF WINE soon turned into three, but none of them did a thing to ease Bob's state of mind. That night, he lay awake in the dark and the quiet for some time before his restless thoughts finally began to grow still. Just as sleep at last began to take him, the dim awareness of a bright light shining against the other side of his eyelids prevented Bob from drifting off. Having drunk himself deep into apathy, Bob did all he could to ignore it at first. Soon, however, the light had grown too intense to pretend it was merely a dream. Slowly–grudgingly–his eyelids unsealed.

What Bob saw made his muscles go tense and his body jerk upright in bed. A white light was present at the foot of his bed. Bob looked beside him to Emily and saw that she was fast asleep and unaware. Bob looked back to the light to find it moving through the air and rounding the corner of his bed to float past him out of sight. As it did, it sent shadows dancing eerily all about the room expanding and contracting, pitching high and low with a distinct but unpredictable rhythm.

Bob turned his head to track where the light had gone, but now, in its place, he found a man. At least, he thought it was a man. It might have been a woman just as easily, for all Bob knew. The short, slender figure that now stood in the corner was oddly ageless and ungendered. It had the bodily proportions of a child, save for its long, muscular arms. Flowing white hair hung down past its shoulders. Its skin was as smooth as porcelain and glowing with the same white light Bob had witnessed a moment before. If not for the plain white tunic and cap the figure wore, both of which dampened its illumination slightly, Bob would have been unable to hold his eyes on the being because of its intense brightness.

"Are you the Spirit who was foretold to me?" Bob whispered into the night. Emily was still breathing softly beside him, well asleep, and Bob would hate to wake her for the sake of a mere hallucination–although in his heart he knew that this was nothing of the sort.

"I am," his guest replied. "I am the Ghost of Christmas Past."

"Long Past?" asked Bob.

"No. Your past."

Bob pulled the covers up over his head. He wanted to fall asleep now–to drop off and find when he awoke that all this had merely been the wine at work in his dreams.

"Why would you hide from what you created?" came the Spirit's voice through the blankets. Its tone was gentle.

"I'm not hiding from anything," protested Bob from below the covers. He stole a peek above to see if the Spirit's voice was still in possession of a body. It was. The bright little person was eyeing Bob with a delicate smile. It seemed in no hurry to move things along.

"What business has brought you here?" asked Bob when he could bear the silence no longer.

"Your welfare," said the Spirit.

"In that case, perhaps you could fix me a drink."

"No," replied the spirit, slightly more stern than before. "I am here for your reclamation. Drink brought you here. Come, let's see the path you have taken."

The Spirit approached the bedside and extended its hand.

"Rise," it said, "and walk with me."

Bob eyed the pale, slender fingers. Then, reluctantly, he shrugged off the blanket, rose, and took the Spirit's hand as instructed. Its grip was gentle but firm. It guided Bob to the bedroom window–the largest in the house. It was just big enough for Bob to walk through in a crouch. The Spirit's child-sized stature had floated out at full height. Now it stood in the foggy abyss outside as though atop some invisible bridge.

Bob lingered on the other side of the window with his feet firmly planted on the floorboards. His arm was stretched outside the sill into the cold of the night, hand still clasped in the Spirit's reassuring grip.

"I'm mortal, Spirit," said Bob, voice shaking. "I'll fall."

"Bear but a touch of my hand and you shall be upheld in more than this," the Spirit replied. Its gentle gaze seemed to bore through his eyes into his soul, filling him with warmth and courage from within. The sensation was so potent that Bob found himself ducking through the open window and stepping out into thin air.

The Spirit had spoken true. The seemingly bottomless ocean of fog beneath him accepted his weight and held him up just as it held up the Spirit. Before Bob knew what to think, the fog was rising around them, whisking them away into the night, sending them higher and higher until at last its gray mists parted. Now, they were soaring above London in the clouds.

Soon, Bob and the Spirit descended back towards London, the city once again coated in a thick, icy mist. The air was cold and biting, albeit not nearly so merciless as it had been during Bob's trek home from the tavern.

They touched down in a narrow court with many tightly packed together buildings. By the light of a flickering gas lamp, Bob saw bold letters painted across the window of a modest establishment across the street from where he and the Spirit now stood. Though Bob could not make out what the letters spelled with his eyes, he had a good inclination in his gut. A strong sense of familiarity fluttered inside him as he took in the surroundings.

"I recognize this place," said Bob.

Before them, a group of older children and younger teens played an evening game of cricket in the street. Bob's eyes widened as he recognized one of the players—a boy in his early adolescence playing outfield on the fringes of the group.

"And that's . . . that's me," Bob realized aloud, for the boy before him was none other than himself as a youth—

thick dark hair, bright blue eyes, and skin a shade paler than his boisterous young companions.

Looking back toward the ghost, Bob noticed that the Spirit alone seemed aware of the present-day, adult Bob's presence on the street. Bob sensed that he, along with the Spirit, were nothing more than invisible onlookers to this moment in time.

"You're half-rat," the young teen up to bat was taunting as he waved his stick, "Cratchit will have to field the play."

"It's gonna fly past yer head and batty-fang your mum," the boy who was pitching jeered back through bared teeth. Though his young self was unfazed, the adult Bob couldn't help but wince at the deluge of swearing.

"You couldn't," the batter taunted back.

"Try me, ya mary," seethed the pitcher, and with that he hurled the ball with all his might straight down the middle. The batter swung and hit, turning the ball into a furious blur that sped through the air right into the window of a nearby establishment.

Bob cringed in unison with his younger self at the smashing sound of breaking glass. His eyes followed the trajectory of the ball until they reached the jagged chasm it had made in the building's storefront window. The group quickly descended into panic as they heard motion come from inside the building.

"Back slang it!" cried the teen with the stick. "Someone's coming!"

Marley
and
Scrooge

Bob saw two tall, imposing figures step out from the shop wearing thick woolen overcoats and expensive top hats. Their fine leather shoes were so well polished that they managed to catch a shine even in the feeble light of the foggy, lamplit street.

"Run! Run!" shouted the pitcher.

The whole pack scattered in a dozen different directions down the street–all except for the young Bob, who remained rooted to his spot in the outfield yelling, "Where are you going? We have to fix this!"

We have to fix this. The adult Bob mouthed the words silently alongside his younger self. All of this was coming back to him as though it'd taken place only yesterday.

The rest of the ballplayers, however, paid no mind to Bob's protests. "Forget it!" one cried.

"No, run!" another yelled.

The youths fled down the street and out of sight. In the absence of any other children to hold accountable, the two men from the shop marched directly over to Bob. Between the shadows cast by their hat brims and high collared coats, their faces were hidden in darkness.

"What have we here?" asked the man on the right. His voice was deep and stern as he swept his top hat off his head, revealing a beaky nose, jutting chin, and bristling salt-and-pepper hair. It was of course none other than Scrooge–still in the middle of his life and yet still an unthinkable number of years older than the boy who stood before him in judgment.

"Tell us your name, young man," said the man to Scrooge's right, his voice cool and crisp. Now he swept his own hat off his head, revealing himself to be an equally younger Marley.

"Bob, sir," said the young Bob. "Bob Cratchit."

"You realize you just broke our window, Mister Cratchit?" Marley said.

"Our new window," Scrooge growled.

"I'm sorry, sir," said the youth.

"See that sign? Marley and Scrooge," said Marley, gesturing to the sign which bore the same names. "That's us. We just had that stenciled on the glass last week."

"It was very expensive," added Scrooge.

"I'm sorry, sir," returned the young Bob. "I take full responsibility." The adolescent hung his head. The words might have been meant as a mere apology, but Scrooge's face perked up at the word "responsibility." A strange gleam sprung to life in his eye.

"You take full responsibility?" asked Scrooge.

"Yes, sir," replied young Bob.

"Did you throw the ball that shattered our window?" Scrooge inquired.

"No, sir."

"Did you hit the ball?"

"No, sir."

"Did you fail to catch the ball?"

"No, sir."

Scrooge and Marley exchanged a look. Their eyebrows were raised slightly, as were the corners of their mouths.

"Well, that doesn't sound very responsible to me," said Scrooge.

"He was part of the game," offered Marley.

"Yes," nodded Scrooge, "wasn't there a group of you? Where are they now?"

"I don't know, sir."

The two men exchanged the same look again.

"Should we turn him over to the police?" asked Marley, not sounding particularly excited by the idea.

"That would ruin his life," said Scrooge, shaking his head. The adult Bob's eyes widened at the words. Would the Scrooge he knew today ever show such compassion to a child? Bob could hardly believe he once had.

"And . . ." the middle-aged Scrooge went on, ". . . our window would still be broken. No . . ."

"Please sir," the young Bob pleaded. "I'll do anything."

The young Bob's mind clawed for ideas on how he'd raise the money. In his mind's eye, he saw himself pawning his family's own meager possessions, scouring garbage piles in the vain hope of finding something valuable, perhaps even turning to thievery. The only thing of value young Bob really had to offer was his own labor.

"I could work it off," he suggested meekly.

Scrooge and Marley exchanged the look yet again. This time, there were full-on smiles on their faces.

"Where do you live, Cratchit?" asked Scrooge.

"Camden Town."

"Mister Cratchit," declared Scrooge, "I expect you in this office at six in the morning to work off the cost of our window."

"Al-alright. I mean, yes, sir." The young man stammered with shock, surprised by both Scrooge's acceptance of his offer and the forcefulness with which he demanded Bob act on it.

"If you are not, I will report this to the police and tell them that a Bob Cratchit of Camden Town has taken full responsibility for it. Do you understand?"

"Yes, sir."

"Six o'clock tomorrow morning sharp."

"Yes, sir. Thank you, sir."

The boy backed away from the men a few tenuous steps, then took off running down the street at full tilt. As he watched his younger self, Bob recalled the light-as-a-feather feeling of relief that had carried him all the way home that night.

The adult Bob and the Spirit remained with Scrooge and Marley on the street as Bob's younger self disappeared into the fog.

"A bold choice, Mister Scrooge," said Marley, highly amused. "I see you've taken my advice to accept more risk in your investments."

"He takes absolute responsibility for his circumstances," returned Scrooge. "That is as stable as an investment gets."

The Ghost of Christmas Past turned and looked up at Bob, blinking its pale, unearthly gaze as if expecting him to comment. After a moment, Bob obliged.

"It seems like so long ago."

"Strange," said the Spirit, "to have forgotten it for so many years. Let us go on."

They took twelve paces across the street to the front door of Scrooge and Marley's establishment. Within that span of time, the sun shot up from the horizon to move over London as throngs of people sped by them in a blur. By the time they reached the shop's facade, a new day had dawned and settled into morning.

They stepped inside the business. Bob's adolescent self had already arrived for his first day of work. Despite draping his coat over the hole in the window to block out the cold as best he could, the youth was still shivering where he sat between Scrooge and Marley in a makeshift desk made up of jagged planks and jutting nails, clearly scavenged from the trash of a less frugal business. It wasn't a very comfortable arrangement, but the makeshift desk and stool were more than sturdy enough to hold the young Bob upright while he worked.

"I worked hard that week," Bob remembered aloud. Learning the meticulous details of bookkeeping had been mentally exhausting, and all the back-and-forth errands Scrooge and Marley had him running for their business was equally taxing on his body. That first week had tested the young Bob's grit, most certainly.

"You were motivated," said the Spirit. "Let's skip ahead, shall we?"

Outside, the sky flickered back and forth from bright to dark like a candle sputtering to stay alight. It came to a halt during a sunset.

Bob scanned the room. Now Scrooge was the only person here, pouring over a ledger at his desk. The broken window had been replaced with a new pane of glass. Looking around, Bob soon found his eye drawn to a large, lumpy envelope lying on the end of Scrooge's desk.

Just then, the teenage Bob tromped in through the front door, still panting from an errand.

"I delivered those letters you asked me to, Mister Scrooge," the youth announced.

"Good," said Scrooge. "Your salary for this week is on my desk." He issued a curt nod towards a large, lumpy envelope laying on the edge of the desk.

"My salary?" asked the boy, his brow furrowed in confusion.

"Yes," returned Scrooge. "It turns out the first glassworker gouged us. Always someone trying to pick a man's pocket."

The young Bob reached out slowly, as if he thought by moving too fast he might frighten the envelope into fleeing before he could take hold of it. His fingers closed around it. It was the first time he'd touched a bundle of wages in his life.

"I don't understand . . ."

Scrooge looked up from his work.

"You worked an extra two days beyond the cost of the window. That should be fair compensation."

Bob overturned the envelope and shook loose its lumps into his open palm. A handful of coins slid out. To a poor boy born in Camden Town, it was more money than he'd ever received in a single sum.

"I'll need the envelope back," added Scrooge. "We reuse those."

"Thank you, sir," the young Bob said. For a moment, he just stood there, mouth agape and eyes wide, taking in the sight of his first earnings. Meanwhile, his adult self looked towards Scrooge, who was looking at the boy. That strange gleam was shining out from the pit of Scrooge's stony gaze once again, only now Bob found that he could place it. It was the same gleam that always manifested whenever his boss pondered a particularly lucrative investment.

"Would you like to earn more money, Mister Cratchit?" asked Scrooge.

"Yes, but . . ." young Bob began, then trailed off. After a pause, he finished, ". . . I don't know how to invest like you or Mister Marley."

"We could train you," Scrooge proposed in his usual unaffected manner, voice devoid of all emotion or attachment.

Bob watched his young face light up.

"I'm not paying you to read, though," Scrooge appended. "You'll have to study extra on your own time."

"But you would teach me?"

"We'll give you meaningful work to see if you are able to learn the business," Scrooge replied.

Now the boy's feet were fidgeting about where he stood, his young body struggling to contain its excitement.

"Oh, thank you Mister Scrooge! I'll be back first thing tomorrow morning!" he exclaimed.

His new boss gave a nod of approval, and with that the young Bob turned and began to bound his way out of the building, nearly skipping in his glee. His first earnings were clutched tightly in his fist, still holding on to the envelope.

"If you keep the envelope," Scrooge called after him, "I'm deducting it from your next salary."

The young Bob halted in his tracks, spun around, and ran back to return the envelope to Scrooge's desk. Then he pocketed his salary and took off.

The Ghost of Christmas Past turned to Bob.

"Did you want to work for Scrooge?" it asked.

"I did," Bob replied. "I thought I could change my life with Scrooge."

"Did you?"

Bob found that no answer to the question came to mind, but the Spirit didn't seem to expect one. The ageless figure began to walk, leading Bob back to the shop's door.

When they stepped outside, it was not back onto the narrow court where Scrooge and Marley's business sat. Instead, they had stepped directly from the business into the living room of Bob's home. The door snapped shut behind them.

The whole Cratchit family was gathered here in front of Bob and the Spirit—Bob himself, Emily, and all their six children—every one of them just a hair younger, enough for them to appear slightly different to Bob. He quickly deduced that he was looking at his family from a year or so before his present self's place in time. Tiny Tim in particular was one year smaller-looking—but one year less sickly-looking as well.

As Bob's eyes drank in the sight of them, the echo of the Spirit's question resounded in his head.

"I suppose I did," he said. "I made a living. I could afford a family."

Tiny Tim was seated in his past-self's lap. The boy's crutch was nowhere to be found. Bob recalled that the crutch came later on.

On this night, Bob's younger self was reading a book to the children, all of whom were enthralled with his enthusiastic performance. They giggled to themselves at the silly voices he put on and laughed out loud at his exaggerated portrayal of the characters. The smiles came so easily to their faces.

For a while, the present-day Bob took in the scene with teary eyes, reliving how effortless good things used to be.

The story he was reading came to a close, and past-self Bob shut the book. Tim slid off his lap and attempted to join his siblings where they sat in a circle on the floor. The first step was sure, the next one rather wobbly. By the third step, the boy began to lose his balance. With the fourth, he was toppling over sideways—right towards the razor-hooked point of a rusty iron poker in its stand beside the hearth.

For a moment, the present-day Bob nearly dove to catch his son out of reflex but, luckily, his slightly younger, slightly sharper self sprung up to save Tim first.

He succeeded in pulling the boy out of his trajectory towards the poker, but he failed to catch him completely. Tim slid against the hard stone floor face first, scraping his forehead. The boy began to cry, and the family rushed forward to comfort him.

The scene blurred forward in time once again. Now Bob and the Spirit were standing in the kitchen with Emily and himself on either side of them, the two of them lobbing hushed remarks back and forth in the aftermath of Tim's fall.

"It's getting worse," Emily said. "Can we afford to take him to a doctor on your current salary?"

"No," said the younger Bob.

"What are we going to do?" Emily asked, volume rising.

"I'm going to have to ask for a raise," replied Bob, staying calm.

Emily's face curled in disbelief at the impossibility of such an idea.

"No . . . Scrooge would never," said Emily.

The younger Bob turned towards the doorway to the living room and called, "Peter! Could you bring Tim in here?"

Peter appeared with Tim as requested. The older boy was holding his hand to keep him steady as he guided him into the room. When the pair of them were near enough, the younger Bob replaced his eldest son's grip as the steadying force for tiny Tim.

"Tim," said Bob gently, squatting down to join the boy at eye level. He gave his little hand a squeeze. "Can you walk from one end of the kitchen to the other?"

Tim looked at him, eyes wide. He nodded as he bit his bottom lip.

"I'll be right here if anything happens," offered Bob, rising up, letting go of Tim's hand, and reaching out his arms to form a protective buffer around the boy.

Tim began to walk with slow, unsteady steps. Bob's past self stayed beside him as he did–arms extended, eyes engaged, reflexes primed to catch the boy at the first sign of collapse. The Bob from the present watched with gritted teeth, tense muscles, and knotted stomach. He braced himself for what he knew would happen next.

"You can do it, Tim," his younger self assured. "I'm right here."

The boy's eyes were welling up with tears at the pain in his legs. Tim was trying his best to be strong and please his father by doing as he wished, but his legs struggled to carry even his tiny frame. Bob wanted desperately to look away, knowing now the pain his son was going through, but his gaze could not be persuaded to leave his son's challenge.

Tim took another trembling step forward. When his foot came down on the floor, it gave way under his weight and twisted in the wrong direction. The boy barreled over, but Bob's younger self was quick enough to catch him before he reached the floor. Tim began to cry.

"I'm sorry, father!" he sobbed. "I'm sorry I couldn't do it!"

"Shh. It's okay," said Bob's younger self, "I'm right here."

He rocked back and forth with the boy in his arms.

"We love you. We're right here for you."

The younger Bob looked up from the embrace towards Emily. She met his gaze with a pointed look that said, "You know what you must do." For his son, Bob was willing to do the unthinkable–he was willing to ask Ebenezer Scrooge for a raise.

Time's tapestry blinked, and now Bob and the Spirit were back at Scrooge and Marley's. The door swung open. Bob's younger self entered. He wore a long, dark green winter's coat and walked with a brisk, determined stride.

Bob marveled at the coat with its quality material and silver lining. Back then, before Tim's health began to fail, he'd had the spare money to buy it from his earnings. Bob had forgotten that he ever owned a garment so fine.

They followed his past self across the length of the building to Scrooge's desk, Bob struggling all the while to keep up with the Spirit and his own person's younger, more spirited pace.

"Mister Scrooge, I need to talk to you," said younger Bob.

Now Scrooge was the spitting image of the man Bob had come to know. His stony face was a good decade harder than it had been on the street, his sharp features many winters more devoid of warmth.

"Yes, what is it?" he snapped.

"It's about our business," replied the younger Bob. "I'm not doing enough of it."

"Oh?" returned Scrooge, eyebrows feathered.

"Yes. I could be working much harder."

A grin crept across Scrooge's thin-lipped mouth.

"That can be arranged."

The younger Bob's chest swelled, and his voice became more firm.

"Now, I don't want busy work. I want to do something of real value to you and this company."

"Of course," said Scrooge. "There are several accounts you could handle. Or would you prefer to package investments?"

"All of it."

"All of it? Why, you'll be very busy if you do that. You might have to work overtime."

"So be it."

Scrooge's bristled brow was in danger of disappearing into the wispy snowbank of his hairline. His cold eyes twinkled strangely towards his employee as the confusion in them gave way to something that seemed entirely foreign to the man's frozen demeanor. The present-day Bob could hardly believe it, but Scrooge almost seemed to be looking at his younger self with some unspoken sense of pride or admiration.

"Very well, Mister Cratchit," said Scrooge, and with that, Bob's younger self turned to leave. Then he turned back.

"Oh, one more thing," he began. "If I'm to do more work, it's only fair that I should be compensated accordingly for it. Wouldn't you agree?"

"Oh . . . I see," said Scrooge. "You want a raise." The twinkle in his eye disappeared–snuffed out like a candle–to be replaced by the impenetrable blankness that Scrooge always donned when there were terms to be negotiated.

The young Bob must have recognized the look and known the terms that Scrooge was looking for. "No," he said. "I want more work, because Mister Scrooge has told me he does not grant raises."

Scrooge nodded his head in agreement at that, understanding the game his employee was playing.

"Clever. And why do you want this extra work?"

The assertive manner Bob had assumed for the discussion deflated. When he spoke, there was a tremor in his voice.

"I have people who depend on me."

Scrooge nodded. Silence. He leaned back in his chair and scratched his chin. His cold gaze roamed around the room. His mouth was pinched.

Then he let out an exaggerated sigh and gave a nod. Bob's younger self had won. At once, his spine straightened itself from a vulnerable posture to a triumphant one.

"Well? What are you waiting for?" Scrooge huffed, clearly not keen on letting his young clerk bask in the victory. "You've got a lot of work to do."

Scrooge scanned the landscape of neatly stacked paperwork on his desk. Then, rather indiscriminately, he reached forward and shoved a three-foot high column of documents towards Bob.

The present-day Bob nearly groaned out loud from the sheer size of the workload at hand. But his younger self only smiled and let out a chipper "Thank you, sir!" before bustling off with the stack.

They followed him back to his cell. As soon as the young Bob took his seat, the machinations of time took up the Spirit's hastened rate. On Bob's desk, candles shrank, sprang up whole and new, then dwindled back to nothing over the course of what felt like mere seconds. Outside, night unfolded into day and back to night at a rate of nonstop change. Bob watched his younger self work through the stack of papers in a blur, disappearing from his chair late at night only to pop back into being at the wee hours of the morning.

"You worked very hard," noted the Ghost of Christmas Past.

"I was expecting a great payoff," said Bob.

"Did that happen?" asked the Ghost.

Bob swallowed. The question had given life to an unpleasant lump in his throat.

Night broke into day, and now the day stayed put. The past Bob ceased to be a blur and with that, Scrooge strode in through the doorway to join the three of them in the seemingly crowded office, walking straight through the Spirit to get at Bob's desk. There, he stood in silence for some time, quite as unnoticed by the younger Bob as the

Ghost stood unnoticed to Scrooge. The clerk was deeply lost within his work.

Scrooge withdrew an envelope from his breast pocket and extended it towards Bob.

"Your bonus," said Scrooge.

At last, Bob snapped out of his trance to take notice.

The younger Bob blinked his eyes, rubbed them, then blinked them again, twice as hard. When at last he convinced himself he hadn't fallen asleep and dreamt this encounter, he reached out and accepted the envelope from his boss.

"Thank you, sir," he said, soft and full of awe.

"I'm surprised you didn't give up sooner," said Scrooge. "You must be very dependable."

Scrooge turned and left the office. Bob withdrew a wallet from his coat and tucked the envelope inside without opening it, too exhausted to revel in his prize. Then he slumped down to rest his head on his desk.

The sound of the front door swinging open met Bob's ears. The noise roused the younger Bob from his stupor, and he looked up just in time to lock eyes with the scoundrel waltzing in off the street.

This occasion was the first time his former self had ever seen this person, but the present-day Bob recognized the man all too well. He was short, balding, and dressed in ragged clothes. His nose was hooked and crooked. His shifty eyes, sallow skin, and gristly unkempt beard gave him the look of a person who was not to be trusted.

"Why, hello, my good man," the seedy fellow said to Bob's past self in a voice as smooth as oil. "Say, is your boss Scrooge in?"

Now sitting upright and alert like a watchman in suspense, the younger Bob asked, "Do you know him?"

"Why, of course! We're business associates!"

The younger Bob squinted at the man, doubtful of his claim. He did not look the part of someone whom Scrooge called an associate. Reluctantly, Bob pointed the man towards Scrooge's desk. The Spirit and present-day Bob followed the man out the side office.

Scrooge looked up from his desk as the visitor approached, Bob and the Ghost trailing behind unseen.

"Fagin!" Scrooge barked at the man. "Where have you been? I've been looking for you for days!"

The present-day Bob glanced behind to see his younger self sigh with relief as he heard Scrooge's welcome. He remembered being glad to learn that this man was indeed an associate of Scrooge and not some untrustworthy street urchin as his appearance suggested. Bob recalled how he had thought, at the time, that this is why one ought not judge a book by its cover. The present Bob, however, now knew that this time, his first impression held true.

"Ah," breathed Fagin, "always in demand." He wrung his hands together as he shifted from foot to foot. Scrooge beckoned him to come nearer with a clawing motion of his finger. Fagin obeyed, following Scrooge into his office. The present-day Bob had to slide past them before Scrooge closed the door, cutting the sound of their conversation off from Bob's office. Glancing behind them once again, he saw that his past self had fixed his attention back on his deskwork and was therefore wholly ignorant of the quiet exchange taking place at his boss's desk.

"One more day late on my loan," Scrooge rasped in a low voice, "and I could send you to debtor's prison."

"Why, Scrooge," Fagin balked, reaching into the folds of his jacket. "That's why I've brought you these fine silk handkerchiefs as payment."

He withdrew a sad knot of tangled material from his jacket. The threadbare scraps of cloth looked neither silk nor fine.

"You'll notice the gold stitching–" he began, but Scrooge cut him off.

"Stop. I cannot accept these rags."

"But sir," Fagin mewed, "silk handkerchiefs resell for six shillings a piece."

"This is an investment firm, not a pawn shop. We don't traffic in stolen goods."

"Why, whatever are you talking–"

Scrooge launched himself up from his desk towards Fagin. In one fluid movement, he was towering over the grubby little man while his cold eyes smoldered with self-contained fury.

"Fagin, the only reason I'm still talking to you is because I expect this conversation will end with my investment being repaid."

Fagin was doing everything he could to shrink away from Scrooge without fleeing the premises altogether. When he spoke, the prior smoothness of his voice was replaced with desperation.

"Well . . . I will need at least a day if I'm to sell these myself."

Scrooge glared at him in withering silence for some time. Then, the anger in his eyes receded and his face took on its usual condescending scowl.

"I suppose you're more likely to get me my money if you're not in a debtor's prison," he conceded.

Fagin bared his teeth in an ugly yellow grin.

"But it had better come," pressed Scrooge. He nodded his head towards Bob's side office at the front of the building. "I just gave my clerk over there a raise, and I don't intend to lose such a sum twice in one week."

Fagin's shifty eyes lit up like lanterns ablaze in the night. They darted toward Bob's cell, eying an opportunity, then back to Scrooge.

"I'll have your money by tomorrow," said Fagin with a reassuring smile. Scrooge did not return it.

"Tomorrow. And not a day later, or I'll have every constable in London searching for you."

As Scrooge prepared to launch into a tirade of threats intended to intimidate Fagin into following through on his payment, Fagin looked back to see past Bob putting on his coat and heading out the door, his work complete for the day.

"Don't worry," replied Fagin, cutting off Scrooge. "Tomorrow."

His mark escaping, he could not afford to stay any longer. Before Scrooge could say another word, Fagin turned and paced out the door, Bob and the Spirit at his heels.

Fagin led them into the street, where the younger Bob was on his feet, trudging towards home, exhausted from a long day of work.

"Why, Mister Cratchit!" exclaimed Fagin as he rushed after Bob. He threw his arm around the clerk in a big, jovial side hug like the two of them were old friends.

"I just heard the most wonderful news!" Fagin went on. "Congratulations on your bonus!"

The younger Bob blinked his sagging, tired eyes. "Oh ... thank you."

"Why yes, Mister Scrooge told me all about it! He even suggested we celebrate!"

Bob's brow furrowed. "That sounds very . . . un-Scrooge-like," he said.

"It's tradition to celebrate!" cried Fagin. "Come, I know just the place."

Fagin gestured in a different direction than Bob's home, then looked at him. The younger Bob paused, his lips pinched, his forehead wrinkled up in thought, unsure which direction to take. The present-day Bob looked on with a frown. Slowly, his past self's expression grew slack as his mind rationalized giving in to the temptation.

What his younger self was thinking came flooding back to the present-day Bob in a rush. His rationale had revolved around Scrooge's perception of this man called Fagin. For if Scrooge truly trusted the man as he appeared to, why shouldn't Bob do the same?

"What could one drink hurt?"

Bob had spent his day evaluating investors. He had taken responsibility for his family's fortune. He'd even taken responsibility for things that were not his own doing. If this man was anything but trustworthy, then he was Scrooge's responsibility, Bob reasoned, not his.

Bob watched his younger self change course as he followed next to the Ghost of Christmas Past.

"Did you know what would happen?" asked the Spirit. Bob sighed.

"It went against my better judgment," he replied. "But I decided if Scrooge suggested it, then it wasn't my responsibility."

The Spirit raised a thin, silvery eyebrow as they followed Bob and Fagin into the darkening streets that led to Camden Town Square.

"Be careful—there are pick pockets all over this square," Fagin hissed in the younger Bob's ear. At his warning, Bob's hand automatically clutched at the fabric of the left side pocket where his bonus resided. The present-day Bob saw the imprint of the money revealed by the gesture. He also watched Fagin's eyes rest on it, as did the eyes of every pickpocket in the square. Bob realized Fagin's warning had been a trick that caused him to reveal the location of his bonus.

Fagin's shifty eyes darted from Bob towards a child standing among a throng of children gathered on the far side of the square. Fagin gave a nod—a distinct tip of the chin that went entirely unnoticed to Bob's bleary-eyed past self–and his young accomplice broke away from the pack.

The boy's pace slowed to a crawl as he came up on the past Bob's heels with the past Bob none the wiser. Fagin turned his head, looked back towards the child from the corner of his eye, and gave another tilt of his mangy-bearded chin towards Bob's right side pocket.

The boy dove for Bob's empty pocket and Fagin, on the other side, fell over Bob as though to swat him off, feigning surprise.

"Look out! A pickpocket!" Fagin screeched, smacking at the boy's cheek with the back of his hand. "Back! Back!"

Bob spun around in shock, directing all of his attention to the child clawing at his pocket. As one of Fagin's hands struck the lad–who was determined to stay put for the beating–his other hand snaked its way into Bob's left side pocket and lifted his wallet with expert finesse. As soon as the wallet was in his clutches, he stopped striking at the boy, and as soon as the blows stopped coming, the boy ran away, his misdirection no longer needed.

The present Bob looked on with mouth agape as his younger self took off after the child. He had been completely fooled by the charade.

Fagin stayed back to rifle through the wallet while his victim gave chase to the diversion. With quick, cunning fingers he plucked the money from inside and folded the wallet back up, leaving the rest of its meager contents untouched. It was perfect timing, for Bob's past self had quickly given up on chasing the boy. He doubled back to rejoin Fagin, who held his wallet outstretched, as though he'd saved it from the pickpocket's clutches amid the struggle.

"Here you go, sir," he declared with deceitful warmth. "I told you. Pickpockets everywhere."

"That thief," snarled the present-day Bob. His lip was curled in disgust—more so towards Fagin or his own foolishness, he wasn't sure.

"You didn't know?" asked the Spirit coyly. The question hardly needed asking. Bob's younger self was overflowing with gratitude to the point where his body could barely contain it. He hopped from foot to foot as he took the wallet from Fagin, exclaiming, "Oh heavens! Thank you so much. You saved me. I didn't see him coming at all—please, let me repay you somehow . . ."

He went to open up the wallet, but Fagin's hand shot out and clasped it shut before he could.

"Please, please!" Fagin protested, as though the idea of Bob rewarding him for his good deed was absurd. "There's no need. Simply sharing a drink with you at Camden's is payment enough."

"A drink where?" Bob asked.

Fagin strolled through the door of the Camden Tavern with a new spring in his step and the young Bob in tow. Bob's past self took in the cramped, crowded surroundings with wide eyes. He took in the assembly of sinister faces brooding over their cups, the unbrushed cobwebs in the corners of the tavern, and the chipped and gnarled chairs and tables strewn throughout the room. All the while, the present Bob could only note how bizarrely out of place his younger self looked here, like a stranger in a foreign land.

"To think there was a time I'd never been in Camden's before," said Bob to the Ghost.

"To think," said the Spirit.

Fagin swaggered up beside them at the bar and roared, "My friend just got a raise! A free drink for everyone!"

The crowded tavern was drowned in the cheers of its patrons. The younger Bob's cheeks went pale.

"Oh no, no no no—I can't—" he began, but Fagin cut him off.

"Bob, it's tradition! When you get a raise, you buy drinks for everyone! A small matter . . ."

Bob took out his wallet, still protesting feebly under his breath. When he opened it and looked inside, his cheeks went from pale to deathly white.

"What's wrong?" Fagin asked.

"I think that pickpocket must have gotten my raise," said Bob. His eyes skimmed the tavern. The patrons were already celebrating their free round. The bartender was already handing out the drinks.

Fagin slid closer to Bob and threw his arm around his shoulder.

"Tell you what," he crooned in Bob's ear. "How about I loan you the money, and you can pay me back next time."

Before Bob could so much as consider the offer, Fagin had pressed a handful of coins into his palm—the very same coins he'd plucked from Bob's purse minutes before.

"That rat!" cried the present-day Bob. His hands were balled up into fists as he watched the scene unfold from his new and enlightened perspective.

His past self couldn't possibly have been more duped. "Thank you, Fagin!" he exclaimed. "I guess I owe you again."

"You do," Fagin affirmed. The scoundrel's beady eyes were roaming up and down Bob's jacket. "That's a nice coat. Maybe I can take it as collateral. Hold on to it till you pay me back."

The younger Bob's eyes darted around the room. "Well, it's very cold out," he said. His hand stroked the fine fabric of the coat, pinching its edge around the buttons so that the exterior's dark green velvet and interior's silky silver lining could both be felt at once.

"Just till you pay me back," Fagin pushed. "I did cover drinks."

The past Bob winced, looked down at his feet, then gave in.

"Alright . . ." he said as he took off the handsome green coat and handed it over. Fagin put it on at once, smiling a tiny, well-subdued smile that nonetheless came across as a big, sick grin to the present-day Bob. That grin was the last grain of sand that tipped the scale.

Bob's temper overwhelmed him, and he lunged at Fagin with murder in his eyes–only to pass right through the man and go flying headfirst towards a new curtain of swirling fog.

Bob felt himself tumble head over heel several times before his body came back down on solid earth. When he rose and looked around, the fog was at his back and his living room stood before him. It was nighttime. Embers glowed in the hearth.

The creaking of a door hinge sounded somewhere in the distance.

"Bob, is that you?" came Emily's voice from the kitchen.

"Yes—" he called back out of reflex.

"—I'm home!" Bob heard his own voice ring out from behind. He turned around just in time to see his younger self step out from the misty abyss and into the room. At the same time, he became aware of the Ghost's diminutive presence by his side. This was still the past—still the same unfortunate night he'd met Fagin, he knew.

Bob's younger self shuffled by on his way to the kitchen, and Bob's nostrils were overwhelmed with the reek of cheap ale. He wondered if he always smelled that way when he returned from a night's debauchery at the tavern.

They followed him back into the kitchen where Emily—still younger and more vibrant—was busy tending to the Cratchit equivalent of a feast. His past self hugged his past wife in a clumsy, drunken embrace. Then he leaned over a steaming pot on the stove.

"What is that?" he asked. "It smells good."

"Just bone broth," Emily answered. "Barely a shred of meat in there."

"It still smells good."

"I'll make you something better if we can afford a roast this week . . ." Emily offered with eyelashes aflutter. Bob's past self looked away.

"Hasn't Scrooge paid you for this week?" she asked, picking up on the shift in Bob's demeanor almost instantly.

Bob watched his past self's face struggle with the choice of lying to his wife. He wondered if his face always grimaced like this when he lied and whether or not his wife could read his contorted expression as the deceitful signal that it was.

But Bob himself, on the other hand, could read his own expression and discern the internal struggle that was written all over his face. To take ownership of his mistake could cost him Emily's approval, his marriage, and more. It was too much to risk.

"No," his past self declared. "He wouldn't give me the bonus."

Bob shook his head at his past self as a feeling of uncleanliness bubbled up inside of him. For the second time that evening, his younger self had refused to accept responsibility for his circumstances. Now, looking on, Bob was ashamed by the lie, but he was outright disgusted by the lack of accountability.

Just then, the pot of bone broth stew boiled over on the fire. Emily was too upset to notice. She had swallowed her husband's words as though they were gospel and flown into a rage.

"Why, that miserly, no good–" she began.

"Emily," protested Bob.

"–how dare he, after all you've done–

"Emily, the stew!"

"–if there was any justice in your office" she raved on, ignoring Bob, "that old humbug would give you extra for all the work you've done!"

"Emily!" Bob cried. "The stew is boiling over!"

Emily turned round at Bob's behest and snatched the pot off the flame with no glove, burning her finger in the process. She let out a sharp yelp of pain.

Bob hurried over to her to assess the damage.

"It's okay," she assured him.

"Let me see," he said. She gave him her hand. Bob wetted a rag to nurse the wound and wrapped his arms around her from behind as Emily brooded over the kitchen fire.

"I know it's not your fault," she told him. "It's that miser Scrooge. You did everything you could."

Here, Bob saw his past self's chin give the faintest of quivers as a pang of guilt swept across his face, his own lie reflected to him.

Suddenly, the present-day Bob's eye was drawn to the doorway to the living room, where the hearth had abruptly sprung to life. Its fire bathed the whole house in a foreboding orange glow. Bob found himself drawn to it. He crossed the kitchen to stand in the doorway.

From where he stood, the living room he saw contained yet another scene from his past. Here he saw Peter, Belinda, and Bob's younger self gathered in a circle around Tiny Tim while the hearth blazed behind them. They were all watching Tim struggle to get the hang of his new crutches. Judging by the chipper way the boy went about it, you could have sworn he'd been given some great gift.

"Thank you, Father!" he exclaimed. "It was very nice and thoughtful of you to get me these crutches till I can get treatment."

Bob's younger self said nothing. His eyes were wide and glassy.

"These are just till he can see a doctor, right?" asked Peter.

The younger Bob's eyes were glazed over like two frozen ponds. Still, he said nothing.

"Don't be sad, Peter," said Tim. "I'll get better soon."

With a frown, Peter replied, "I think you're going to need a miracle, Tim."

Tim thought for a moment.

"Then I guess I'd better go to the church and pray."

Bob noticed the Spirit standing at his younger self's shoulder. As Bob watched, the Ghost looked past him to the kitchen. Bob followed the path of its gaze into the kitchen where another moment in time was taking place.

Bob saw his younger self hunched over the counter, body racked by dry, heaving sobs. He appeared to be fighting back tears. As Bob watched, his past self fumbled through the cabinets and eventually withdrew a bottle of cooking wine from one, a wood cup from another. He filled the cup to the brim.

"This was when it began," came the voice of Christmas Past, who'd returned to the present Bob's side.

"It wasn't my fault!" he protested.

"Was it your fault when Scrooge's window was broken?" the Spirit asked.

"No."

"Yet how did you respond?"

Bob's younger self downed the drink in two great gulps. He took a deep breath. Then he poured another cup. The present Bob's stomach churned.

"Spirit, I cannot bear to see this," said Bob. "Please, take me away from here."

"These are shadows of things that have been," said the Ghost. "That they are what they are, do not blame me!"

Bob's younger self choked and spat up half the cup. His body gave a great drunken lurch as he made to lean over the counter, coughing. A terrible creaking sound filled the room, and then Emily appeared on the staircase behind him.

"Spirit, please, I cannot take any more of this! Wake me from this dream," pleaded Bob. He turned to look the Spirit in its eyes, but he wasn't met by the Spirit's misty stare. In the Spirit's eyes, Bob saw all of the people he had disappointed. His boss, his wife Emily, and even his son Tiny Tim somehow stared back at him from within those dark circles.

Scrooge's face gave one of his withering looks.

"You were a poor investment," came Scrooge's voice. Its icy timbre seemed to resonate in the space around Bob from all directions.

Emily's crestfallen visage peered out at him from behind the Spirit's mask.

"You let us down," her voice called out from everywhere at once.

Tiny Tim's enormous blue eyes looked up at him from the vessel of the Ghost, wet with tears.

"You failed me," said Tim's voice. The words cut like a knife and felt like they came from somewhere deep within Bob's own soul.

Bob was unable to bear this torture–it had to end! Desperate, his hand shot out and seized the Spirit's cap, yanking it down over Tim's haunting eyes with all his might. Much to his surprise, he was met with no resistance. The cap slid down over the Spirit's eyes and on down past his head. In an instant, the garment had unfurled past the Spirit's feet, hiding all its brightness beneath the white fabric.

And with that, the cap sagged and crumpled over–suddenly quite empty. Shocked, Bob picked it up and looked inside.

An endless, black abyss was staring back at him from inside the cap. Bob leaned forward, entranced by the absence of material where the cap ought to have ended. He leaned forward even more, trying to make sense of the universal impossibility he was seeing, forward more and more until he'd leaned in so far that–suddenly–Bob found himself surrounded by the cap on all sides like a tunnel.

A light sprung to life before him at the tunnel's end. Bob crawled towards it. The light became closer, shining brighter. Just as it grew so bright Bob was certain it would blind him, he emerged from the tunnel and into the comfort of his bed.

The cap's material had turned into sheets. The light at the end of the tunnel had turned into beams of sun. They were flooding into the bedroom through a gap in the curtains.

STAVE THREE

BOB PEERED BACK under the sheets. The tunnel he'd crawled through was gone. The past was behind him once more. The Spirit's torment was over.

Bob dropped the sheet, leaned back, and let his body go limp in bed.

Emily stirred beside him, her entire body hidden beneath the blankets. Instantly, the memory of his younger self lying to her came flooding back to mind. A guilty flutter took wing inside his chest like a bat trapped in his ribcage.

"Emily," Bob whispered to the wife-sized lump beside him, "I have something I have to tell you."

The mound of blankets gave a tiny, indistinguishable grunt. Bob took it to mean that she was listening. He went on.

"Do you remember when I told you Scrooge hadn't paid me? The first time, I mean. Well, I know it's a bit late, but I was lying. He had paid me."

Bob heard the faint sound of birds chirping from outside the window, punctuated by the tinkling laughter of children from elsewhere in the house. Unless his ears deceived him, the kids were already awake. It seemed he and his wife had slept in late. Bob went on.

"The truth was, I lost the money. It wasn't my fault though, a pickpocket . . ."

He trailed off for a moment, realizing he was about to make another excuse for his actions. Yes, it was true his money had been stolen, but the point of sharing this story was not to defend his actions, Bob reminded himself. It was to tell her the truth. He pressed on with his confession.

". . . but it wasn't Scrooge's doing," he concluded, awkwardly. "I just wanted to tell you that."

"Bob, who are you talking to?"

Bob sat bolt upright and looked around. The question had been asked in Emily's voice, but it hadn't come from beside him. Her voice had come from downstairs, calling up to Bob from the kitchen. And that could only mean that the person bundled up in blankets beside him wasn't his wife.

Bob turned his head back to look at the blanket-covered mound curled up to his right. Slowly, muscles tense, he reached out and grasped the top of the blanket. Then he pulled it back.

"Oh, Mister Cratchit!" boomed the merry-faced man lying in wait underneath. "You know just what to say to wake a man up."

Bob jolted back and fell off the bed with a hard thump. The man let out a rumbling laugh. Bob scrambled back to his feet as the stranger in his bed cast aside the bedclothes and rose as well.

The stranger's physique seemed to swell in size as he stood. By the time he reached full height, the barrel-chested mountain of a man positively dwarfed the bedroom with his presence. He wore an exquisite green robe with white fur trim about the collar and sleeves. A circlet made of holly sat atop his brown-haired head, and a regal beard framed his broad, rosy face. His dark eyes twinkled down at Bob as he flashed a pearly smile.

"Well, gaze upon me," he said. "You know who I am, don't you?" The man had both the air of a king and the manner of a child—dignified and boisterous all at once. Indeed, Bob had a good inkling who he was. That didn't mean he was happy to see him.

"Are you . . . the third portly gentleman?" asked Bob.

"No!" the Spirit bellowed in return. "I am the Ghost of Christmas Present!"

"Oh no, no more spirits," said Bob, his voice full of dread.

"Be of good cheer, Mister Cratchit!" thundered the Ghost. "It's Christmas Day!"

Bob sighed. "Spirit . . . Let's get this over with."

The Spirit leapt atop the bed with a nimble little hop. It extended a velvet-sleeved arm within Bob's reach.

"Touch my robe," he commanded.

Bob obeyed. When he did, the world turned into a whirl of color around them. When it stopped, they were standing on a crowded street somewhere in London. A light flurry of snow was falling from above. Bob wrapped his arms around his body to shield himself from the cold.

The Spirit lifted its hand and a torch appeared in his fist. The Spirit gave it a shake, and the torch's crown sprung to life with a flame that was pure blue in color. In the fire's presence, Bob's layer of clothing suddenly felt sufficiently warm for their venture.

With that, they were off—the Spirit wading down the street with great long strides, Bob nearly jogging at its heels to keep up. Despite the multitude of people filling the street, wherever the Spirit went, there just happened to be enough open space to accommodate it. For Bob, however, the same could not be said. The crowd bumped and jostled his body this way and that. Unlike with the Spirit of the Past—during which Bob had been as much a specter to the world around him as his host—it was evident by all the knocking around he was getting that he was back in London in the flesh.

When Bob finally managed to catch up with the ghost enough to walk beside it, he saw that its eyes were flitting back and forth from face to face among the people they were passing on the street, its own bearded face beaming brightly all the while. One after another, each person's manner lit up to reflect the Spirit's dazzling smile.

The Ghost of Christmas Present paused outside a tea shop where a pair of men were seated at a table, sipping steaming mugs with distant, dreary expressions. The Spirit tipped its torch towards each of their cups in turn, a luminescent incense sprinkling out from the flame. At once, the two men burst into highly animated conversation, joking and laughing with one another like old friends. Bob heard the clink of their cups knocking together in toast as the Spirit led him onward down the street.

"Your torch . . ." said Bob, amazed. "What incense is that?"

"It's my own special blend," the Spirit said. Bob noticed that the smoke coming off the torch was oddly shiny and silver in color, not dull and gray.

The Spirit led Bob off the street and down a gloomy side alley, barely wider than his office back at Scrooge and Marley's. Here, half a dozen beggars were huddled around a trash fire crackling in a barrel. They were munching on stale bread with bitter looks on their faces, each doing his best to ignore the other's company. The Spirit dashed some of his incense into their fire, and suddenly they were all eating on their bread heartily as though it were a feast fit for a king. The beggars began to chat with one another in between bites, visibly savoring every mouthful of bread. Bob was in awe of their shift in disposition.

"How can you make these people happy when they have so little?" he asked.

"I give them gratitude, which is worth more than any worldly treasure," replied the Spirit.

The alley led them to the steps of a run-down little church with a sagging roof. The structure's sole Christmas decoration was a lavish wreath–lush and green and swathed in crimson ribbons–that hung from the door. The Spirit led Bob inside.

The vast church was nearly empty, except for a frail, familiar-looking little boy sitting near the front, deeply focused in prayer.

"That's my son, Tim!" Bob exclaimed.

"Where did you think he would be," said the Ghost, "other than his Father's house?"

Bob followed the Ghost up the main aisle, passing row after row of empty pews. As they walked, Bob noticed a gleaming trail of vapor wafting up from the prayers of his son, Tiny Tim. It had the same appearance as the smoke streaming off the Spirit's torch.

"That looks like your incense," said Bob.

"It's the main ingredient," replied the Spirit.

As Tim prayed, the Spirit's "ingredient" streamed out from his mouth. Bob watched the silvery smoke float up to the rafters and pool into a cloud within the pocket of the chapel's bowed-in ceiling. From there, it wafted out in all directions, dissipating back into the church at large.

"That boy has less than most, but he is a thousand times more grateful," noted the Spirit.

Tim closed his prayer with a solemn "Amen," and his great blue eyes opened up. He looked around, sensing another presence in his place of worship, and he quickly caught sight of Bob.

"Father!" he cried.

He slid off his pew, crutch in hand, and hobbled towards the aisle, more excited than his feeble legs could carry him. The boy managed to make all of three steps before he began to teeter over. Bob rushed forth and scooped him up.

From behind him, the Spirit's voice came ringing in Bob's ear: "If you saved half of what you spent on drink to care for this boy—"

"Silence!" Bob shot back at the Spirit. He wanted to connect with his son, not dwell on his failures. Bob decided it was his turn to lead the way. If today was about the Ghost of Christmas Present, then they should do something to celebrate Christmas in the present!

"Tim," Bob said to his son, "we're going to get the Christmas goose now. Would you like to come get the Christmas goose with me?"

"Of course, Father!" Tim replied.

Bob threw the boy over his shoulders and carried him back down the aisle towards the doors of the church. Christmas Present followed, standing directly behind Bob.

"I knew if I prayed, you'd come," Bob heard his son say as the boy looked over Bob's shoulder. His voice was soft and full of wonder.

"Why of course, Tim," said Bob. "Dad is here."

Although Bob had never heard his son address him with such reverence, he knew Tim's comment must have been addressed to him. After all, who else was there? They were entirely alone, and it's not like his son could see the Spirit which followed him.

Bob glanced back at the Spirit. It had on an oddly knowing expression on its face—a strange and more subtle smile than the big pearly grin it had worn before.

A quick jaunt to the tavern and Bob's hard-won goose was retrieved. They were back home in short order. Bob entered his home with Tiny Tim on his shoulders and the Christmas goose in his hands, the invisible Ghost of Christmas Present trailing behind them.

He surveyed the room. His wife Emily prepared dinner in the kitchen dressed in ribbons, and his two children, Belinda and Peter, played in the living room. As Bob smiled at his family, he heard the Spirit's voice whisper from behind.

"Be grateful for the family you have, Cratchit, for not all may be here next year."

The words sent a dread crawling down Bob's spine. He set his son Tim down on the ground as his knees became weak under the weight of the boy and the Spirit's words. When he looked upright again, Bob noticed an empty chair with the shawl of his oldest daughter near his two present children.

"Where's our Martha?" Bob called out, realizing her absence.

His wife Emily was already in motion to him from the kitchen.

"Not coming," answered Emily, her eyes downcast.

"Not coming!" Bob cried. "Not coming upon Christmas Day?"

Emily did not answer. Bob twisted round to look at the Spirit, reconsidering its warning with fear in his heart. Had something happened to Martha? Did the Spirit's words mean he would never see her again?

Just then, a choke of laughter from Emily's direction sent Bob's attention spinning back to look towards his wife. She was giggling, as if his fearful reaction was the intended result of a practical joke she was in on, but he was not.

With Emily unable to keep her composure, the door to the broom closet swung open and Martha stepped out to reveal she had been hiding there the whole time. She ran forward into Bob's arms, seeing that her absence might have rattled him a bit more than intended.

"Don't be sad, Father!" she said, reassuring him. "I'm here! We were just playing a joke on you!"

The whole family laughed as she ran into his arms. Emily appeared at his side and kissed his cheek while the other children hugged him wherever they could reach.

"Martha hid when you came in. She wanted to surprise you," Emily explained.

"I didn't like seeing you disappointed," added Martha. "It was only a joke."

"Oh Martha, I'm so glad you're here," said Bob, relief washing over him. He looked around at his family. Deep gratitude filled his heart. Whatever else happened this fateful Christmas, they were all here, safe and together.

"You know I'd do anything for you!" Bob told them.

A sweet aroma filled Bob's nostrils. It was not the hearty smell of something edible, but the fragrant scent of incense.

Bob recognized the smell. He looked up over his shoulder. Sure enough, he saw the Spirit in the act of leaning its torch over the group, a sly smile on its face.

Bob opened his mouth to address it, but just as he did the children all began dragging him down towards the floor to play by the hearth. Meanwhile, Emily returned to the kitchen with the goose.

Soon, all the meal's preparations were complete, and the Cratchit family was gathered around the goose at the dinner table. The bird was barely bigger than a pigeon. It would have made a filling meal for two people at most.

"I'm sorry that's the largest we could afford this year," Bob told the rest with a hollow voice. "Hopefully it will be enough."

Bob looked around the table. His wife and children wore tired expressions. It made each of them look older than they were. Then, a glimmer of incense rained down from above and all their eyes lit up.

"Bob, it's perfect!" Emily assured. She turned to the children. "Thank your father for getting the goose this year."

The table erupted into praise.

Bob's guilty grimace slowly turned into an uneasy grin. He gave the Spirit a grateful nod for its help. Then he poured himself a drink and lifted it up towards the Spirit, hoping it would dispense another dash of incense into his wine. Instead, the Spirit's kindly eyes grew cold.

"You could have afforded the largest Christmas goose in London without a single bar tab," it said.

Bob looked back at it, frowning. He opened his mouth to say, "What do you mean by this?" but the Spirit answered the question before he could ask it.

"You're an accountant. Run the numbers. You drank your family's feast."

A scowl that would have put Scrooge out of business flashed across Bob's face. Defiantly, he lifted his cup all the higher and defended his drink, saying, "What would Christmas be, without some Christmas cheer?"

His family, who of course had no idea who Bob was talking to when he said this, squinted across the table at him with puzzled expressions.

"Christmas cheer?" asked Tiny Tim.

"Does that drink bring you cheer?" asked the Spirit.

"Yes," Bob replied to the Spirit, "Christmas cheer."

"I'd like some Christmas cheer too, Father," said Tim, offering his cup for some wine.

Bob looked from the Spirit to his son, surprised by the boy's interjection. "You're not mature enough to drink yet, Tim."

"But Father, I love Christmas," Tim pleaded.

"If you are not grateful for what you have," said the Ghost, "it will affect not just you, but your whole family."

"I told you," Bob snapped back at the Spirit, "I need my drink."

"Fine, Father," said Tim tearfully, thinking Bob's words were meant for him. "I will wait until you think I'm mature enough for Christmas cheer."

Emily gave the boy a comforting pat. "Bob, why did you have to tease him like that?" she hissed.

"I was just trying to explain why . . ." he began, quite irate, but his anger quickly faded with the realization he'd been arguing out loud with a bearded, torch-wielding giant that was visible only to him. He resigned himself to glare silently at the Ghost instead.

"Don't look at me," the Ghost said back. "I'm not the one who said Christmas cheer was drinking alcohol."

Tiny Tim hadn't touched his plate since Bob snapped at him. The boy was slumped over in his seat, head hung, sniffling lightly. Bob felt a twinge of guilt in his stomach as he looked at him.

"Fine," he said, reaching for the bottle at the center of the table. He filled a spare cup halfway to the brim with wine. "Here," he said, clunking the cup down in front of Tim. The boy's eyes went wide with surprise.

"Oh, thank you, Father!" he cried. Bob threw the Spirit a smug look, pleased to think the Ghost was not the only being in the room capable of lifting moods.

"Bob!" Emily cried, her face contorted with shock.

"What?" he cried back. "What do you want me to do?"

"I didn't want you to give him a drink!"

"Don't worry, father," interjected Tim. "I promise I will be mature enough to be worthy of Christmas cheer."

"Hey, Father," Peter called from across the table with a sly, adolescent grin, "do you think I'm mature enough for some Christmas cheer?"

A few minutes later, everyone at the table had a cup of wine placed before them—all six of the Cratchit children, young and old. Bob even managed to cajole his way through Emily's disapproval to serve her a cup as well. Having downed two cups himself by this time, Bob was feeling in high spirits. He poured himself the last of the bottle and found himself smiling idly at his family, glad to be with them.

"Merry Christmas to us all, my dears," Bob announced. "God bless us."

"God bless us!" his family echoed back.

"God bless us, every one!" cried Tim, above the rest.

They laughed. Bob reached out beside him to hold Tim's hand, small and frail.

"Ah, you are grateful for something," remarked the Spirit. "For your family."

Bob nodded. His gaze was fixed on Tim.

"For Tiny Tim," noted the Spirit. Its voice fell to a whisper. "Is it because you fear losing him?"

Bob's throat went dry. He twisted around in his chair to fix his eyes on the Spirit. The Spirit wasn't looking back. Its dark eyes were staring across the table towards the wall as though looking off into some distant future. When the Spirit spoke, it was not to Bob directly. It appeared to be addressing a presence unseen.

"I see a vacant seat in the poor chimney-corner and a crutch without an owner, carefully preserved."

Bob felt the color drain from his face.

"If these shadows remain unaltered by the future," continued the Spirit, "none other of my race will find him here."

Bob shook his head in disbelief, but he could not shake the truth he felt in the Spirit's grim prediction. He looked towards Tim, whom he knew was not long for this world if the present state of things continued down this path.

Bob took comfort in the fact that it was still an "if" and not a "when." He racked his brain for a way to change the Spirit's vision. An idea came to mind. Back in the rundown church where he'd met up with Tim, the Spirit had hinted that gratitude was the main ingredient for its magic. The ghost had said that Tim was more grateful than most, despite having less. What, then, was an area of lack in his life he could try to be grateful for?

Bob leapt up to his feet and raised his cup. "A toast!" he proclaimed.

His family looked at him, befuddled by his erratic behavior.

"To . . ."

Bob reached through the deepest recesses of his mind for the most unlikely thing to be grateful for.

". . . Mister Scrooge! I'll give you Mister Scrooge, the Founder of the Feast!"

Emily balked. "The Founder of the Feast indeed!" she cried. "I'd give him a piece of my mind to feast upon, and I hope he'd have a good appetite for it."

"My dear, the children," pleaded Bob. "Christmas Day." He gestured towards the Spirit, though they could not see it.

"It should be Christmas Day," Emily snapped back, "I am sure, on which we drink to the health of such an odious, stingy, hard, unfeeling man as Mister Scrooge."

Bob opened his mouth to protest, but Emily shot him down before he could speak.

"You know he is, Robert," she said. "Nobody knows it better than you do, poor fellow."

"My dear . . ." he urged. ". . . Christmas Day."

His wife shook her head. "I'll drink to his health for your sake and the day's, but not for his. Long life to him. And a Merry Christmas and a Happy New Year!"

She raised her cup in toast. The rest of the family followed suit, children lifting up their wine half-heartedly and uncertainly. The gesture Bob had meant as an offering of gratitude rang hollow through the house.

"He'll be very merry, I have no doubt," added Emily. "I don't like it, not one bit."

The children made their best attempts at choking down the wine that Bob had set aside for them. Peter alone made no indication of offense at the dark red liquid, while Tiny Tim's face scrunched up like a prune from the moment the wine met his lips.

"I don't like it," he said, coughing, "not one bit."

The Spirit put a hand on Bob's shoulder, and he noticed its knuckles were sharper than before, its fingers more gnarled. Looking back at the Ghost, Bob saw that a gray tinge had crept into its beard.

"Did you think feigning gratitude for Scrooge could earn your son's health?" the Spirit asked. Bob considered the question for a moment, then replied.

"I just wish I had more to give this Christmas . . ."

"I'm grateful we only have a little," Tim responded, drawing Bob's attention from the Ghost.

"Why do you say that?" asked Bob.

"Because it makes each bit more precious," Tim replied.

"But what if this was our last Christmas together?" Bob choked, his throat closing up at the thought of it. "What if someone couldn't make it next year?"

The boy pondered the question with an innocent look, as though Bob had merely asked him why the sky was blue instead of red. He narrowed his eyes and rubbed at his chin, as children often do when they're thinking hard. After a pause, he offered up the answer he'd worked out.

"If we only have a limited time together, then each moment is a reason to be grateful."

Bob sat for a spell with that reply. The whole family did.

"I'm grateful to know you, Tim," said Bob, breaking the silence. "For however long God gives me."

In his heart, Bob felt a deep and profound gratitude for all the moments God had given him with Tim thus far. And although he knew the moments yet to come may be fewer than he'd like, Bob felt blessed beyond measure to know that there were more to come at all.

Just then, a knocking sounded at the door.

Bob wondered who that could be. Emily's puzzled expression seemed to ask the same. Bob looked towards the Spirit for an answer but received only a grin and a shrug.

Bob left the table to answer the door. A burly man holding a large, oblong-shaped delivery wrapped in thick brown paper greeted him from the step.

"Delivery for Bob Cratchit?" asked the man.

"That's me," Bob replied.

The man thrust the package into his arms. It was warm—almost hot, and weighed more than Tiny Tim.

"Merry Christmas, sir," said the man. "Someone must be looking out for you." With that, he turned and disappeared into the flurry of snow that was overtaking London.

Bob returned to his family with the package, placed it down on the table, and unfastened the string that held its wrapping. A plume of steam rose up from inside as the package shed its crinkly shell. The Cratchit family gasped.

Sitting before them was the largest, most succulent-looking, most delicious-smelling turkey they'd ever seen. The children's gasps quickly turned into shrieks of joy.

"Bob!" rang out Emily's voice, adding to the chorus of delight. "You didn't tell me you were getting us the prize turkey!"

"I didn't!" Bob admitted. "Who is this from?" Once again, he looked towards the Ghost of Christmas Present for an answer. The Spirit's only reply was to erupt into a fit of booming laughter. Bob cocked an eyebrow, as if to ask the Spirit, "Did you do this?"

"What are you waiting for?" Emily called out. "Carve the turkey, Bob!"

Bob shook off his confusion over the turkey and set about the task of carving and serving it instead. It was no small ordeal. The bird was so large that Bob wasn't quite certain how to tackle cutting it into edible portions. He sawed off what he could, improvising as he went, and soon he'd placed a piece of meat on Belinda's plate that was bigger than her head. The whole family laughed.

A second round of dinner commenced, and they all gorged on the turkey in a state of sheer bliss. When it was over, Bob suspected that his children's stomachs had never been quite so full.

They retired to the living room. Martha lit a blaze in the hearth. A bag of chestnuts made its rounds while they all sang Christmas songs. With Emily and the children all lost in their singing, the Ghost leaned in next to Bob and said:

"Tell me—did you have more joy in your heart before or after the prize turkey arrived?"

"It was . . . the same," Bob realized aloud. "I was grateful when it arrived, but the joy was already there before it arrived at my door."

Bob sat in silence for a moment, thinking hard on his new revelation. A question for the Ghost bubbled up in his mind.

"Is your Spirit really the same everywhere?" he asked. "No matter how much a person has?"

"Yes," replied the Ghost without hesitation. "The same in rich and poor."

"How can that be?"

The Spirit reached out its arm.

"Come. Take my robe."

Bob looked back towards his family then to the Spirit's outstretched sleeve. The Ghost gave a reassuring nod. In the Spirit's eyes, Bob saw that his family would not be disturbed by his absence.

Bob took hold of the robe, and they were off. The Cratchit carol gave way to the roar of whooshing wind as their feet lifted off the ground and the light moved around them.

When their movement ceased, Bob found himself entering a lavish, densely occupied ballroom. Finely woven tapestries depicting Christmas fables hung from the manor's twenty-foot-high walls. Here, there was not one but *four* hearths burning, two on either side of the massive ballroom chamber where Bob and the Spirit now stood. There were easily over a hundred guests mingling with each other in high spirits, all clothed in formal suits and frilly dresses. Here and there, trays of cream-filled French pastries bobbed through the crowd, carried by servants.

Though Bob had never been here before, he knew at once where he must be.

"The Lord Mayor's house!" he exclaimed. "Surely this is the greatest Christmas party in all of England."

Nearby stood a group of partygoers gathered around a woman who could only be the Lord Mayor's wife. She was a thin and sickly-looking woman who at one time might have been fat, for her skin hung loose and empty off her like grisly curtains. For the festive occasion, she'd adorned herself with many strings of large and opulent rubies across her emerald-colored velvet garb. Her body was so frail, however, that the oversized jewelry only seemed to weigh down her entire physique as though she were a prisoner in chains. In her face, too, it was as if the great weight of her finery dragged downward all her features. The corners of her mouth settled in a deeply etched frown, and likewise with her eyes, which gave her a most beady and mistrustful sort of countenance.

Among the guests standing about the Lord Mayor's wife were the two portly gentlemen who'd solicited Scrooge for a donation that Christmas Eve. Bob recognized them at once. As he looked on, a confection-laden servant approached the group and offered them a pastry. Each of the gentlemen's eyes went wide with delight as they sampled a morsel from the tray.

"It's so sweet!" said one.

"The sweetest pastry I've ever had!" said the other.

"It's too sweet," said the Lord Mayor's wife, making a sour face. She tossed her half-eaten pastry back on to the tray. "This is a disaster. Take these back."

"What would you like me to do with them, miss?" the servant asked.

The Lord Mayor's wife rolled her eyes. "Enshrine them in tinsel. What do you think? Throw them all out."

The servant gave a nod and attempted to leave, but the portly gentleman immediately protested at such a great waste.

"You can't be serious?" one said.

"But they're so sweet!" the other added.

The mayor's wife merely shrugged.

"They're all yours if you like them so much," she said, looking down her nose at the two men. "You can have all the disaster pastries you want."

The gentlemen exchanged a look, a gleam in both their eyes.

"All of them?"

A few moments later, Bob and the Spirit were tailing the two portly gentlemen up the lamp-lit lane that led to the Lord Mayor's house, Bob careful to linger a good distance back so as not to seem suspicious. The two men were wheeling a cart piled high with "disaster pastries."

The gentlemen walked with a bounce in their step all the way to the other end of town. At last they came to a dilapidated building in London's poorest district. The two men disappeared inside. After a moment, the Spirit slipped in after them with Bob in tow.

Within the building, men, women, and children of every age gathered around a crackling hearth singing Christmas carols. One would never know all they had to eat was simple porridge by the joy with which they raised their untrained voices in a chorus of hymns. Many a small child was among them. Bob realized this place was a house for the poor.

Despite the disheveled state of the poorhouse's inhabitants and the paltry excuse for a Christmas dinner on their laps, Bob sensed a feeling in the air not so different from the one within his own home, prior to leaving with the Ghost of Christmas Present. Each among these unfortunate souls ate their porridge with as much enthusiasm as Bob's children when they ate their turkey. Bob could see that these people were grateful to be eating at all—and doubly so to be eating in a warm room surrounded by their loved ones.

The first portly gentleman stepped into the building empty-handed. The awareness of their presence quickly spread among the group, all of whom met their arrival with a chorus of cheers and applause.

Bob watched one sunken-faced man clap the shoulder of a small boy to his right—a frail little lad no older nor more vigorous than Tim by the look of him.

"Those men are the reason we have a meal tonight, son," Bob heard the man tell the boy. "This is their house we are staying in."

"God bless you, sirs!" the boy cried out, and Bob was reminded of Tim more than ever.

The first portly gentleman raised a hand to quiet the group. "Now," he said with a statesman's air of importance, "we are not here to provide you with any more dinner this evening."

He paused. The group looked on at him, still smiling. It was clear they expected nothing more from the men, so grateful they were for what they'd already received. The gentleman continued.

"We are instead here to provide you with dessert!"

The second gentleman stepped outside, then reappeared—wheeling the cart piled high with the pastries. The group at large released an excitable gasp, marveling at the beauty of the treats, which then broke into cheers. The people approached, and the sweets were distributed into their hands with many an expression of thanks.

Looking around the room, Bob saw satisfied smiles spread across the faces of the people as they bit into their treats. Many made audible sounds of pleasure at the taste. Others split their treats into portions to trade amongst themselves so that a variety of the pastries could be sampled by all. Each bite was savored, every last crumb regarded with the awe and admiration befit a precious jewel.

Bob watched the small boy who reminded him of Tim sink his teeth into a sweet. His eyes lit up with awe, and at once Bob saw in his face the proof of what the Spirit had claimed–gratitude really was here, and in equal measure to the homes of the more privileged.

"The Lord Mayor's wife thought these were too sweet!" chortled one of the gentlemen. "Too sweet! Have you ever heard such a thing!"

Everyone laughed. The whole room was beaming. Bob turned around to look at the Spirit and found its bearded face was no exception.

"Such joy!" Bob remarked.

"Not for the Lord Mayor's wife," said the Spirit with a wink.

"Why could she not experience it?" asked Bob.

"Why can a camel not pass through the eye of a needle?" asked the Spirit in return.

The question made Bob pause, though no answer he could find.

"Merry Christmas, everyone!" called one of the gentlemen. Cries of "Merry Christmas!" flew back at him from all directions in return.

"I wish I could do as much good as these gentlemen have," said Bob, still fixated on the Tim-like boy's enormous smile.

"There is something," said the ghost.

"What?" asked Bob. "I have no money to give them."

The Spirit reached out a sleeve. "Come."

Bob touched the garment.

The gentlemen and their charges vanished, the walls around them fell. Now they were standing on a jagged cliff overlooking the ocean. A terrible storm raged on the horizon. Thunder boomed in Bob's ears. Wind whipped at his hair.

"What is this place?" Bob yelled over the thunder and the wind.

"This is what those numbers you move around all day actually represent," the Spirit bellowed back. It took Bob's hand and led him off the cliff to stand on naked air—just as the Ghost of Christmas Past had done before. Together, they drifted down to the base of the cliff. Here, the splintered, half-sunken remnants of a ship were ensnared amidst its rocks. Dozens of barrels bobbed in the salty brine around the vessel, their contents ruined by the sea.

They floated from the ship's untimely grave to a nearby stony shore where the survivors of the crash were gathered, huddled around a sputtering flame that burned against all odds in the dark, stormy night. As Bob and the Spirit floated closer, he could just barely make out their voices over the roar of the wind.

The crew of this shipwreck were singing Christmas carols, the same song as those in the poorhouse and with just as much joy and spirit in their voices.

"They seem so happy, even though they've lost their whole ship," noted Bob.

"As happy as the poorhouse was before dessert," said the Spirit with a nod.

Bob examined the survivors. He had worked with Scrooge long enough to know a man of finance when he saw one. He saw sailors, cooks, a captain, but no such man of finance in the group.

"There's no insurance officer among them," said Bob. "Was this venture not insured?"

He looked back towards the wreckage of the ship and the rock face that had doomed it. Bob knew when a vessel was insured, the insurance company typically placed an officer onboard to ensure proper safety was followed. They couldn't have the crew cutting corners to save money that would risk the cargo, knowing insurance would cover them if their cost-saving shortcuts led to ruin. The insurance officer might better be described as the safety officer, ensuring all proper procedures were followed, yet this vessel had none. That could only mean one thing.

"They must have taken shortcuts with safety and wrecked," said Bob. "A firm like ours could have prevented this."

As he spoke the words, they sparked a revelation in his head.

"I could have prevented this," he corrected.

The Spirit looked at him with gleaming eyes. "And you do," it said, "every day at your work. Be grateful, for here is where you can do much good."

It smiled. As it did, the tinge of gray in its hair and beard spread, then turned to white. Its kingly stature sagged; its ox-like physique turned to flab. The wrinkles in its face spread out like sprawling vines on an old abbey wall.

"Come," the Spirit wheezed. "Our time grows near."

Bob took hold of the Spirit's robe a final time.

The Spirit's magic brought them back to the threshold of Bob's home. In the flash of time it took to go from the shore to Bob's front step, the Ghost appeared to have aged another ten years. Now it had the shrunken, stooped over stature of a man in his final twilight.

"Are all spirits' lives so short?" asked Bob.

"My life upon this globe is very brief," the ghost replied. "It ends tonight."

"How can you accomplish your work in such a short time?"

"I dwell within the homes of all who call upon me this day."

"It is truly a Christmas miracle that your spirit of Christmas can be all around the world at once," said Bob, impressed.

"The real miracle is that every mortal manages to be exactly where they need to be with only one body and one life."

They stepped inside. Most of the family had gone to bed, but they found Emily washing dishes at the sink. Tiny Tim was at the dinner table, nibbling on a piece of leftover turkey. Both were so engrossed in their activities that neither looked up and saw that Bob and the Spirit had entered. Then again, they wouldn't be able to see the aged Spirit even if they had noticed Bob, or so he thought.

"Are there others who can see you like I can?" Bob asked the Spirit in hushed tones, not wanting to disturb his wife or son just yet. Regardless, Tim looked up and over toward where his father stood beside the Spirit.

"Every child who believes can see me. And those they pray for."

The Spirit took a step back. As it did, something poked out from under its robe. Bob looked the Spirit in its eyes, his brow furrowed.

"Forgive me, Spirit, but is that a foot . . . or a claw?"

Whatever it was, it slunk back under the robe just as Bob noticed it.

"It might be a claw, for the scant flesh there is upon it," said the Spirit. "Look here."

The Ghost of Christmas Present shifted its robe to the side, and two small, child-sized figures scurried out into the kitchen, rattling the floorboards with their rapid footfall.

Bob spun to track where they were going. He turned around in time to see two blurs disappear beneath the table. With a great storm of clamor, they jostled past the table's legs, bumping and spilling drinks on the surface above. Tim seemed not to notice, simply staring off into the distance, unable to see these creatures or any effect they had on the room around him. An impish cackle that seemed part child and part beast echoed from underneath the table, as the thrashing of furniture filled the room with a series of clattering sounds akin to the rapid bursts of canons fired quickly in succession.

Emily called from the kitchen. "Is everything alright in there?"

"Yes," Bob replied. "Stay in the kitchen!" He did not want her endangering herself by approaching whatever monster the Spirit had allowed to crawl into his home.

"We're fine!" Bob added, as he rushed to where the creatures disappeared under the table. "Don't come in here."

The creatures reappeared at the other end of the table, each climbing into a chair across from Bob and the Ghost of Christmas Present. Bob saw that they were two thin, dirty children dressed in tattered rags—a boy and a girl. Their hair had the mangy, matted texture of a feral dog's fur. Their skin had the sickly, sallow look of a leper's complexion. Where youthful innocence should have lit their features, they had been twisted and pulled into shreds, so the space in their soul where angels might have sat enthroned, devils lurked, and glared out menacingly.

Neither Tim nor Emily—still washing dishes at the counter—gave any sign they could see the ghastly creatures. Bob turned to the Spirit, seeking explanation, only to find the ghost had aged another ten years since he last looked away. Its withered skin was wrinkled like old parchment. Its snow-white beard was but a few wispy tufts on its chin. Bob found the Ghost's decrepit look concerning, but he was even more concerned with the two fearful figures it had unleashed into his kitchen.

"Spirit," Bob began. "Are these your children?" he asked.

The Spirit's throat rattled as it gave its reply. It was the wheezing, rasping sound of someone at death's door.

"They are Man's. This boy is Ignorance. This girl is Want. Beware them both, and all of their degree, but most of all beware this boy, for on his brow I see that written which is doom."

"Spirit, why do you let them dwell at my table?" asked Bob, fearfully. "Have they no one to care for them?"

"Don't you know?" the Spirit replied. "You have been feeding them for quite some time."

The Spirit pointed back towards the table. Bob looked back and saw Want sitting beside his son Tim. The boy tried to eat, but every time he lifted a piece of turkey to his mouth, Want grabbed it from his hands and devoured it first. Tim ate and ate, but could never fill himself, because each time the fiendish little girl behind him would take the meal he intended for himself. Tim was none the wiser.

"Stop it!" Bob yelled at Want, "That's my son's food!"

He leapt forward and seized hold of Want.

"Am I not the child you have raised?!" it hissed.

The creature writhed in his arms, kicking and scratching Bob with all its might. In his struggle to subdue the creature, Bob knocked Tim's plate off the table. It fell to the floor and shattered into pieces with a crash, scattering Tim's food. Tim didn't even look at it. Instead, he merely stared straight ahead, eyes glazed over as though in a trance.

Bob's face contorted in anger that in his attempt to protect his son's food, he had destroyed the whole meal. He prepared to strike Want and shift the blame of his own actions entirely onto the creature who caused him to take them, when Want looked right into Bob's eyes, perhaps even past them into Bob's soul, and told him who was really to blame.

Want let out an ear-splitting cackle. "Every drink that took food from Tim's plate nourished me," it screeched.

The truth of the creature's words stung Bob. His anger gave way to guilt and then shame as he realized that however demonic the messenger, it had spoken the truth, and its doing was his own.

The creature seemed to delight in his pain, letting out another ear-splitting cackle. The shock both of realization and the creature's disturbing reaction caused Bob to lose his grip on Want, allowing it to break free and scurry back under the table out of sight.

Just then, another crash from the other side of the kitchen commanded Bob's attention. Looking over to the sink, Bob saw the wretched boy called Ignorance crouched on the counter, whispering in Emily's ear.

"Yes, yes . . . it's all Scrooge's fault," Bob heard his wife mutter, repeating whatever lies it was pouring into her ear. "He's the reason for what happens in this house."

Bob dashed forward to separate Ignorance from his wife, but as he did, Want reappeared by Tim's side. Desperately, Bob looked back and forth between the two, then toward the Ghost of Christmas Present.

"Spirit, please!" Bob cried, pulling at his hair. "Take this away from me! I will hear whatever you have to say!"

The kitchen clock chimed. Its face read twelve.

A torrent of pitch-black fog poured into the kitchen from the living room. It brought with it a chill that snuffed out every candle. Darkness filled the room.

STAVE FOUR

THE PITCH-BLACK FOG surrounded Bob from every side. All at once he was alone in a dark and endless void.

Gradually, Bob's eyes adjusted to the light—or lack thereof. Out of the void, he saw a tall, man-shaped figure gliding towards him. Its body was cloaked in a robe of deepest black, which left nothing visible of its head or face or form. Indeed, it took all the might of Bob's eyes to discern the figure from the blackness of the never-ending void in which it stood.

A dread sunk deep into Bob's stomach, like a cold void within him that mirrored the dark space surrounding him. A part of him felt as though it recognized the approaching being in a strange, distant way.

The hooded figure extended an arm that was draped in a tattered sleeve.

"Are you the Ghost of Christmas Future?" Bob asked.

The spirit was silent. Its bony hand pointed downward.

"You're not going to talk, are you?" said Bob.

The Spirit nodded.

"You're just going to show me terrifying things and offer me no words of comfort," Bob said, vocalizing his fate. By now, he knew the nature of Spirits. He did not look forward to his final haunting.

The Spirit said nothing. Slowly, it stretched its skeletal hand out ahead of them, pointing it forward into the void.

"Oh, I could really use a drink right now," Bob sighed.

The Spirit cocked its head to the side, as if to ask if such desire was really an appropriate response given all Bob had learned through his visions.

Bob inhaled deeply, preparing for the journey ahead. "I'm ready," he declared through gritted teeth. "I'm ready. Lead on."

The Spirit hovered forward, legs–if indeed, it had any–hidden beneath its billowing, pitch-black robe. The void around them thinned back into the rolling cloud of smog that had laid claim to Bob's kitchen.

The smog dissipated further, finally giving way to the sight of a soot-covered London street beneath a steel-gray sky. An imposing stone building made up of columned grandeur loomed before them. A flock of well-dressed men in top hats were gathered around its steps like a court of stately crows.

"Wait, I know this place," said Bob. "Is this . . ."

The Spirit paid him no mind. Instead, it hovered onward up the great stone steps between a pair of pillars and into the building itself.

". . . Yes, it is the London Exchange!" exclaimed Bob, making haste to catch up with the Spirit. He bound up the stairs and crossed through the columns. Soon he had arrived beside the Spirit in the building's grand interior, panting slightly.

Here, the top-hatted fellows were gathered in a boisterous swarm of commerce. Traders and businessmen shouted their bids as others tracked the changing prices or huddled in groups to negotiate private dealings. The whole scene formed a cacophony of flowing money.

"Spirit," Bob gasped. "Do you realize you've taken a trader to the stock exchange of the future?!"

He took in the stock prices with wide, hungry eyes. "Do you know what I could do with this information?!" he exclaimed. "Quickly!"

The Spirit remained silent as Bob desperately looked around for something with which to record the lucrative numbers he heard and saw. Coming up short of a paper and pen, Bob set himself sprinting through the exchange, mumbling the more significant-looking figures he saw thereabout under his breath, determined to memorize all he could on the spot.

"Two and quarter . . ." he breathed. "Forty-five . . . three, and–oh, I wouldn't have expected that! Down ten, I'll have to remember to avoid . . ."

A familiar figure cut across the crowd, overtaking Bob's concentration.

"Is that . . . Scrooge?" Bob breathed. His heels skidded to a halt on the spot.

It was indeed. Scrooge, more or less as Bob had known him from the present, was snowy-haired and dressed in all his subtle, well-fitted finery. Bob turned back to look for the Spirit in the crowd, only to discover it had reappeared by his side. Its ghostly lantern eyes shone down at Bob in a way that made his arm hairs stand on end.

"Spirit, what is he doing here?" Bob asked. His voice held the inkling of a quiver. "The London Exchange was supposed to be my responsibility."

Over the years, visiting the Exchange with a list of stocks to sell and buy had become a routine task on Bob's list of clerical errands. Why would Scrooge, who positively loathed the company of his colleagues at the Exchange, ever go back to running such an errand himself? The Spirit offered no explanation. It said nothing.

"Do you hear me, Spirit?" pleaded Bob. "Where am I right now?"

Just then, another familiar figure stepped out from the throng of top-hatted traders. It was one of the two portly gentlemen, albeit significantly less portly than when Bob had last seen him alongside the Ghost of Christmas Present.

"Ah! Mister Scrooge!" the gentleman exclaimed. "It's a pleasure to see you again!"

Scrooge gave the man a stiff nod. "You as well," he replied flatly. Bob edged his way closer to the men to better hear their words over the building's roar and bustle.

"I think I've seen you here every day this week!" declared the gentleman.

"My investments never stop working. Why should I?" Scrooge returned.

The gentleman gave a jovial nod. "Doesn't it get tiring? My associate and I take turns working the exchange."

Scrooge ground his jaw as he fixed his icy gaze off in the distance. "I had an associate once," he mused.

"Oh yes, I think I remember meeting him. What was his name?"

"Bob!" interjected Bob himself. "Bob Cratchit!"

Neither Scrooge nor the gentleman appeared to hear him.

"It's not important now," said Scrooge. "He is no longer with us."

Bob looked back toward the Ghost with mouth agape.

"Spirit, what has happened to me?" he asked. "Do I no longer work for Scrooge?"

The Spirit was silent.

"How do I care for my family?" pleaded Bob. "For Tim? What happens to his care?"

Slowly, the Spirit turned and stretched out its hand, gesturing back towards the door from whence they had entered the Exchange. The Ghost drifted towards the door. Bob followed it outside the building and then beyond into the London street.

The gray sky gave way to nightfall as Bob trailed the Spirit through the cold city's depths. Despite the darkness encroaching on Bob's vision, the route they were taking felt intensely familiar.

"I know this way," said Bob. He looked up at the dark, looming specter as he walked. "Spirit . . . are you taking me to my house?"

Sure enough, at that moment they rounded a corner and stepped onto Bob's street. After a few moments more at the heels of the Spirit's brisk pace, Bob was climbing the crumbling stairs of his own front step. The Spirit passed through the door to his home. Bob followed suit.

Inside, the house was dead quiet, save for the last few embers of coal that were crackling in the hearth. Peter sat in a corner, reading a book by the dying fire's dim light. In the other corner, Emily, Martha, and Belinda sat knitting in silence. All of them looked older.

As Bob took in the scene, Peter read out from his book mid-story.

". . . And he took a child and set him in the midst of them."

On the other side of the room, Emily sat her needlework down in her lap and rubbed her face. "The color hurts my eyes," she said.

Bob moved closer to his wife. With every step, new lines in her face were made visible by the light of the fire. When he was close enough to touch her, Bob reached out a hand in a gesture of comfort. She didn't respond.

Bob pulled back his hand, startled by her non-reaction. Then he remembered, just as with the scene from his past that the first Ghost had shown him—this was not his time; his presence was not felt.

"They're better now," Emily went on, still rubbing at her eyes. "It makes them weak by candlelight, and I wouldn't show weak eyes to your father when he comes home for the world. It must be near his time." She lowered her hands from her face and straightened her posture in the chair.

"Past it, rather," said Peter. He shut his book. "But I think he's walked a little slower than he used to these last few evenings, Mother."

For a few moments, the whole room was as silent as the Ghost that hovered by Bob's side. When at last Emily broke the silence, her words were strained.

"I have known him to walk with–"

Her voice faltered, and Bob's stomach sank as he realized she was fighting back tears. His heartbeat quickened with fear. He perceived that something in this house was very off.

Emily cleared her throat and, composing herself once again, pressed on.

"I have known him to walk with Tiny Tim upon his shoulder very fast indeed," she said. She smiled as if choosing to focus on the joy of that memory rather than a heavier burden which lay on all their hearts.

"And so have I often," said Peter.

"And so have I," added Martha.

"And so have I," agreed Belinda.

"But he was very light to carry," said Emily. With that, she snatched up her needle and resumed her knitting with renewed intensity, desperate–it seemed–to be lost in it. Bob looked towards the Spirit with dread.

"Spirit . . . what are they talking about?"

The Spirit said nothing. Emily's attempt to distract herself with knitting, meanwhile, proved futile. She spoke up again.

"And his father loved him so, that it was no trouble," she said. "No trouble."

With that, the horrible truth that hung unspoken in the room dawned on Bob. A gasp passed through his lips.

"No . . . it can't be . . . "

Just then, Bob heard the sound of creaking hinges behind him.

"And there is your father at the door," said Emily. She dabbed at the corner of her eye with her knitting, stood, and forced her mouth into a smile.

Everyone, including Bob, looked towards the door to see Bob's older self enter the house, still trembling from the cold. Compared to the Bob watching the scene, this man's cheeks were more hollow, his brow more creased, and his eyes more sunken. The beginnings of an unkempt beard clung to his jaw.

Emily, Belinda, and Martha all walked over to embrace him. After their greetings had been given, Emily set off to fix Bob's future self some tea while the girls returned to their needlework.

"Your knitting looks quite good, girls," the older Bob said as Emily returned and pressed a steaming mug into his hand. "Very–very productive." He sipped his tea. The present-day Bob could sense something out of place in his older self, a lack of cheer in his demeanor that could not be waved away by mere tiredness.

"Sunday," Emily said. "You went today then, Robert?"

"Yes, my dear," the older Bob replied. "I wish you could have gone. It would have done you good to see how green a place it is." His shaggy chin gave a quiver. His eyes were wet. Then he bit his lip, as if to hold back the display of emotion that was trying to escape, and the quivering stopped.

"But you'll see it often," he told them. "I promised that I would walk there on a Sunday. My little, little child. My little child!"

All at once, the older Bob burst into tears.

As Emily and the children all rushed forward to comfort Bob's future self, the present Bob's gaze turned from his family to the chair by the fire–the chair where Tiny Tim had once so often sat. Then he fixed his gaze on the Spirit.

"Spirit–how could this happen? How could my son Tim die?"

The Spirit did not reply.

"Please Spirit!" shouted Bob. "Show me, now!"

The fire in the fireplace went out, plunging the room into darkness.

A few coals sputtered back to life then grew into meager flames. Its light revealed that the scene had changed–now Bob's future self sat alone before the hearth, staring blankly into the fire with a flask in his hand. A layer of unshaven stubble clung to his face. An empty chair sat across from him on the other side of the hearth.

Behind him, the front door swung open, and Tiny Tim hobbled in on his crutch.

As Bob watched, the boy inched his way across the room to where Bob's older self sat by the fire. Each slow, rickety step was a greater struggle than the last.

"You were here when I left to pray today, Father," said Tim, reaching Bob's older self at last. He placed his crutch in its usual place beside the hearth, then climbed into the chair across from his father. Bob's older self was silent all the while, his eyes fixated on the fire. The flames were beginning to dwindle.

"Aren't you cold without a coat?" Tim asked.

The older Bob shifted in his seat and muttered, "I had a coat once." He took a swig from his flask. His gaze did not leave the hearth.

"You mean when you used to work for Mister Scroo–" Tim began.

"What have I told you," the older Bob snarled.

"I'm sorry, Father, I know you don't like that name. I don't like it either. I know he's the reason we can't get my medicine anymore."

"That's right," growled the older Bob. "It's all his fault. Him. Scrooge." He downed another swig from his flask and pondered the dying coals' depths. The present Bob could make out the reflection of the embers in his future self's glassy eyes.

"At least we can still afford your medicine, father," offered Tim.

"His fault," muttered Bob's older self. "His fault."

"It's okay, father. I know that whatever happens to me, God will use it to teach others."

At last, the older Bob turned his head to look full-on at his son.

"I love you, Tim," he whispered.

"I love you too, Father. You know I pray for you every day at the church. I pray for everyone."

His father lurched forward off his chair and flung his arms around the boy. The flask went flying into the dark.

"No, please," cried Bob's older self into the crook of Tim's neck, "Please don't go yet."

"Why do you say that, father?" asked Tim. "I'm right here. My crutch is over there. I couldn't leave if I wanted to."

The older Bob wrapped his arms around the boy even more tightly, holding him close. A stream of tears shone from either cheek.

"No, please," he whispered, "please, please . . ."

"What's wrong, Father?"

Bob's older self let out a sob, then slumped back into his chair. Tiny Tim began to shiver.

"Father, can we put another coal on the fire? I suddenly feel very cold."

Bob's older self did not reply.

"Father, did you hear me? I wanted to know if we had another coal for the fire. Father?"

The older Bob's tear-addled eyes returned to the hearth. As the last ember faded, he rose and left the room. Tiny Tim called after him through chattering teeth.

"Where are you going? Can't you hear me, Father? It's cold. I feel cold. It's so cold."

The boy stopped speaking. His eyes went wide.

"Oh, it's you."

Bob realized Tiny Tim was looking directly at the Ghost of Christmas Future.

"You weren't the spirit I was hoping for," Tim said, "but I knew you were the one who was coming." He rose from the chair and walked towards the Spirit–walked with the gait of a perfectly healthy boy, like he had never needed a crutch in all his life.

As the boy grew near, he looked the Ghost directly in its shrouded face.

"I'd like to meet my heavenly Father now."

The Spirit reached out its bony hand. Tiny Tim took it. The two of them turned and walked together towards the door. It swung open of its own accord as they drew near, and the pair stepped forth into the abyss of snow and fog that lay beyond. They vanished.

Now Bob was alone in the room. He turned and looked back toward the hearth. Tiny Tim's body was still in the chair, ghostly pale with limbs hanging limp. His chest was unmoving. His eyes were shut. No breath passed through his lips. Death had taken him.

Bob screamed.

"NOOO!"

He took off sprinting towards the door after the Ghost, launching himself into the void of fog and snow.

"Spirit! Spirit, where are you?!" he cried.

Somewhere in the distance, he heard the ticking of the clock–though he couldn't determine its source. All Bob could see was the ground beneath his feet and the icy veil of mist that hung around him on all sides. Off in the distance and behind the curtain of mist, he could just barely make out the Spirit's dark, slender shadow. Bob ran harder, and the shadow grew larger. At last he reached the Ghost.

"Spirit!" he demanded, panting. "Where is he? Where is he?!"

The Spirit lifted its arm and pointed onward through the mist. As Bob followed its skeletal finger, the wall of fog around them receded enough for Bob to make out their surroundings.

They were standing in a graveyard. The Spirit was pointing towards a headstone, small and plain. Following the Spirit's finger with his gaze, Bob read upon the stone the name TIM CRATCHIT

"No, Spirit!" pleaded Bob, falling to his knees on the hard, frozen earth. "Please, no . . . this is so much worse than if it were my own grave."

He looked up toward the Ghost. Behind the Spirit and the fog, Bob could see the immense silhouette of the cathedral where Tim had so loved to pray.

"There must be some way to prevent these horrors, Spirit!" Bob cried, reaching out and clawing at the tattered hem of its robe. "Please show me! How can I avoid this future?"

The Spirit moved its hand from the grave to point off in the distance. As Bob's eyes followed, the fog cleared there as well. In its absence, Bob saw himself running through the snow down the street–not his older self, nor his younger, but himself exactly as he was when he last looked in a mirror. Bob also saw Christmas decorations on the buildings around him, and the bustling crowds of people returning back to business from their holiday.

"Spirit, is that me?" asked Bob. He stood bolt upright from where he had collapsed at the foot of the Spirit's robe. "Tomorrow?"

The Spirit said nothing. Bob watched his tomorrow-self run.

"Am I late for work?" Bob pried.

The Ghost was silent.

"I am, aren't I?"

Bob saw his future-self trip over a crate in the street and go tumbling down onto the cobblestone. As he scrambled to his feet, a grim realization dawned on Bob.

"Scrooge will fire me," he said aloud. He looked toward the Spirit.

The Spirit nodded. Once more, it extended an arm. This time, however, it wasn't pointing toward something for Bob to see. Instead, the Spirit seemed to be offering Bob its tattered sleeve. Bob reached out and took hold of the pitch-black fabric. It was unexpectedly soft.

All at once, the Spirit took off, Bob clinging to its cloak. His heels were lifted off the ground as the Ghost became a dark blur that shot through the graveyard at inhuman speed. They weaved between headstones, flew over graves, and sped around statues. In a few chest-pounding moments, they had arrived at the street. In a few more, they had overtaken the tomorrow Bob as he sprinted for work and dear life. They rounded a corner and arrived at Scrooge's place of business well ahead of him.

The pair of them slowed and drifted through the storefront, coming to a stop just inside. Relieved, Bob relinquished his white-knuckled death grip on the Spirit's cloak. He felt his feet anchor themselves to the earth once more.

They stood outside Bob's side office, awaiting the arrival of the late Bob who had to live this vision. Across the front door, Scrooge was sitting at his desk, pondering the sight of the clock that was ticking on the wall. Its face read nine eighteen. A triumphant grin spread across Scrooge's thin lips. The sight sent a chill down Bob's spine.

"Oh no," Bob gasped, his voice unheard by his boss as before.

Bob's tomorrow-self bolted inside the building and sped into his cell–chest heaving, red in the face, and brow glazed with sweat. In his mad dash to slip into his office unnoticed, he forgot to close the door behind him. An icy gust followed him towards his desk and after that–Scrooge.

"Hallo," rasped the latter, arriving at the door to the cell and making the tomorrow Bob jump a foot in the air off his stool in surprise.

"What do you mean by coming here at this time of day?" demanded Scrooge.

"What do you mean?" answered the tomorrow Bob, voice straining to feign surprise. "I've been here all morning. I'm not late, if that's what you're implying." The present Bob winced at his brazen display of dishonesty.

"You are," refuted Scrooge. "Yes, I think you are. Step this way if you please."

Bob's tomorrow face took on a defiant scowl. It made Bob look more ugly than he'd ever seen himself.

"Look–it's not my fault," the tomorrow Bob protested. He crossed his arms. "There was nothing I could do. You're always so bah-humbug all the time . . ."

Bob's tomorrow-self must have taken note of the way Scrooge's bushy brow furrowed–the narrowing of his eyes, the venomous flash of anger that gleamed behind his frigid stare–for the clerk backtracked almost at once.

"I mean," he stammered, "I didn't mean to say that. It's not my fault. You–you made–"

Scrooge cut him off.

"Now, I'll tell you what, my friend. I'm not going to stand this sort of thing any longer."

Bob's tomorrow-self's body seemed to shrink where he sat. Bob saw a lump run down his throat as he gulped. His face contorted.

"Wait!" cried the clerk. "Don't fire me! I need this job! Tiny Tim's life depends on it!"

Scrooge ignored him, pressing on, "And therefore–"

"No!" shouted Bob.

Before Scrooge could finish, light filled Bob's vision and the vision flashed from his eyes as his scream rang out into a blind void.

STAVE FIVE

BOB'S CRY ECHOED off the ceiling of his bedroom.

He sat up and took in his surroundings. He was back at home in his bed. Emily's half of the mattress was empty with blankets strewn to the side. Sunlight was streaming through the window.

"It's morning," Bob realized. "I can still change these visions." He looked out the window at the rows of snow-capped rooftops and whispered, "Thank you, Spirit."

Suddenly, the abrupt awareness of a ticking sound took hold of his attention. His eyes darted to the clock on the wall.

"I'm late."

Without a second thought, Bob threw off the blankets, rose, dressed, and took off for work. In the blink of an eye, he was running down the street at full tilt—just as he had witnessed himself at the side the Spirit.

Ahead of him, the crate he'd seen his future-self trip over lay in the road. He leapt over it with a nimble jump.

"Ha!" he exclaimed, neck craned to look back at the vanquished obstacle as he sprinted onward down the road. "I didn't trip! I can change it! I can change—"

He turned his head back around just in time to see the wooden face of an overhanging shop sign, half an inch in front of his nose. He crashed into the sign face first and was knocked back off his feet.

Head throbbing from the blow, feet struggling to find traction on the slick blanket of snow, Bob scrambled back to his feet and took off running again, humbled but not defeated by the unforeseen collision.

A few blocks later, Bob was racing through the threshold of Scrooge's building—once again too exhausted to notice that he'd left the door wide open in his wake. Bob shed his hat and scarf as he entered and, without a glance toward Scrooge's desk, he made his last mad dash into his cell and plopped down on his stool.

"Hallo," croaked a voice at Bob's back a moment later. "What do you mean by coming here at this time of day?"

Bob's posture stiffened where he sat. He recognized the words as exactly those from his earlier vision. Thus far, his day was proceeding as it had before. He was late. He had fallen on his journey to work. Now, Scrooge had caught him. Unless he changed something, he would set in motion a new chain of events that would lead to a future he could not bear.

Bob remembered the lesson of his visions. He took a deep breath, paused, then turned around to face his boss. He knew he could not drown this in drink, nor shift the blame to someone else. He had to be honest about what had happened, perhaps even grateful, and resolved to take ownership even if the outcome was beyond his control.

"I'm very sorry, sir," said Bob as he locked eyes with Scrooge. "I am behind my time."

Something was missing in Scrooge's stare as he returned Bob's gaze. The menacing glint Bob had seen in his vision was absent. When Scrooge spoke, the harsh edge he had harbored in his voice was absent as well. His words themselves, however, were the same.

"You are? Yes, I think you are. Step this way, if you please."

Bob nodded expectantly. This time his protestation was firm, but calm.

"It's only once a year, sir. It shall not be repeated. I was rather merry yesterday, sir."

Scrooge went on as though he had not heard him. Again, his words were familiar.

"Now, I'll tell you what, my friend. I am not going to stand this sort of thing any longer. And therefore . . ."

Bob took a deep breath and braced himself for what he knew was to come. In his visions, Bob saw himself respond with bitterness and contempt towards Scrooge. Instead, he felt a warm sensation rise in his heart that he could not explain, which could almost be described as gratitude.

". . . And therefore, I am about to raise your salary," Scrooge finished.

Bob's body lurched backward so hard, he nearly fell off his stool. He looked up at Scrooge with eyebrows high and mouth agape. Scrooge looked back with a smile.

"A Merry Christmas, Bob."

Scrooge strode across the length of the cell, approaching Bob's desk. And as he walked, Bob observed a lively spring in his step that had never been there before.

"A merrier Christmas, Bob, my good fellow, than I have ever given you for many a year. I'll raise your salary, and I'll endeavor to assist your struggling family."

Bob was stunned into silence. His thoughts were a jumble, and his throat was thick. Scrooge closed the gap between the door frame and the desk and clapped his clerk on the shoulder.

"And we will discuss your affairs this very afternoon, over a Christmas bowl of smoking bishop, Bob."

With a parting pat on Bob's back, Scrooge made to leave the office. At last, Bob found his voice.

"Mister Scrooge, I . . . I don't know what to say."

Scrooge turned and fixed Bob with a look that was vaguely reminiscent of his old icy glare—save for the addition of a merry glint that shined behind each eye.

"Make up the fires," he ordered in a mock-stern tone, "and buy another coal-scuttle before you dot another 'i,' Bob Cratchit!"

Scrooge reached into his pocket and took out a coin. He flipped it across the cell with a wink. Bob caught it.

Moments later, a slightly bewildered but very grateful Bob was bundled back up in his hat and scarf and making his way down the street towards the nearest coal merchant. At the end of the street, parked on the corner, was the same gin cart that had peddled its wares outside of Scrooge's establishment only two days prior, as long ago as that seemed.

"Hey, you there!" the owner of the cart barked at Bob.

Bob ignored him, but the vendor persisted.

"You! Can I interest you in a drink?"

"No, thank you," Bob replied.

"You sure? Christmas special!"

"It's not Christmas anymore."

"After Christmas special!"

"No."

The salesman looked nearly as confounded by Bob's new disinterest in gin as Bob had been by Scrooge's newfound generosity.

"You've never passed this cart without a drink before," the vendor protested. "Found another buyer, have you?"

Bob shook his head and said, "I've had my fill of spirits."

The gin seller scowled. Just then, a ragged-looking child ran up to the cart and proclaimed, "I'll take a drink!"

And before the salesman could reply, the little urchin snatched a drink right off the cart.

"Stop, you little thief!" the vendor cried.

The child had turned, intent to take off, but Bob seized him by the scruff of his collar.

"Let me go!" screamed the child.

Bob had not stopped the boy from running off to protect the gin seller's business. In truth, he had recognized the little thief.

"You work for Fagin, don't you?" demanded Bob.

"Not anymore. Fagin's dead."

Bob frowned, though not out of pity for the scoundrel's passing.

"Where are his things?" Bob asked the thief. "I have a debt to settle with him."

"Probably buried with him in a pauper's grave."

As they were speaking, the gin salesman had ambled around his cart to stand over the urchin threateningly, his fists clenched.

"Where would that be?" Bob pressed.

"By the church in Camden Town," yelped the lad, eyes darting back and forth between Bob and the cart vendor. "Now let me go!"

Bob let the boy go. He took off running at once. The vendor glowered at Bob, but Bob barely noticed. He was already striding off, course set for the old cathedral and its graveyard.

Soon he arrived at the cemetery gate. There hung above it an old wooden sign. As Bob drew closer, the image carved upon it came into focus. Bob paused when he saw what was engraved on the sign's face—a hooded reaper in the spitting image of the Ghost of Christmas Future.

Bob stared, marveling at the sign. Only the sound of singing in the distance broke his state. Beyond the gate, Bob saw the glint of a shovel flinging dirt up over the edge of a hole from within. As the unseen digger in the hole slung back the dirt, he warbled out the likes of a crude tune in time with his labor.

"Brave lodgings for one, brave lodgings for one, a few feet of cold earth for when life is done."

"Hello?" interjected Bob. He had made his way across the cemetery and approached the open grave while the man sang. Now that he was close enough to look down into the hole at the gravedigger's features, Bob almost wished he hadn't. The digger was a short, ill-looking fellow whose dirt-covered clothes seemed more miserable than he was. The man had a shrunken-down, withered sort of look to him, one that brought to mind an image of the last sad leaf that clings to its tree well past the onset of winter.

"Is this the service for Fagin?" asked Bob.

The man let out a hollow laugh.

"Service. That's a good one. Yeah, I perform a service. It's called cleaning up after the hangman."

The gravedigger climbed out of the grave and planted his shovel in the earth alongside the spread of tools and bags that were strewn across the ground in a pile. Among them was a cheap bottle full of cheaper alcohol.

"Where is everyone?" asked Bob, as the man leaned over his things and picked up a bottle.

"No one ever comes here but me and this old wicker bottle," answered the man. He reached for the bottle and took a swig.

Bob scratched his chin, pondering over the scant few details he knew about Fagin.

"But there were so many who knew him," Bob remarked. "Children even."

"Guess they didn't know him that well," returned the man. Then he leaned forward with a knowing grin on his face. "Or maybe they did."

Bob peered over the edge of the hole into the grave. A handful of man-sized lumps were piled in a heap at the bottom. Each was wrapped up in a white cloth, browned slightly from the dirt.

"The name's Gabriel, by the way," said the man as he bent over to set his wicker bottle down. He straightened back up. "Gabriel Grub."

With that, he stepped to the side of the grave where another man-shaped, cloth-wrapped lump was lying in wait for its final destination. The gravedigger seized it from one end and said to Bob, "Help me with this, would you?"

Bob hesitated. His last visitation to this place alongside the Ghost of Christmas Future was fresh in his mind.

"Wait, shouldn't we say a few words before burying him?" Bob asked Grub. It seemed wrong to simply dump the body without any kind of ceremony of some kind. The gravedigger stared at him. Bob realized the man was waiting for him to perform last rites as he was the only other person present, and he began to stutter.

"Oh, uh . . ." Bob searched for something meaningful to say. "Lord . . . Holy Spirit–Spirits . . . we pray that you give this man rest, and . . ."

"Amen," Grub cut in. He hoisted his end of the body and swung it over the edge of the grave. Bob scrambled to get a hand on the other side.

The body plopped into the hole with a dull, sullen thud. Grub dusted off his hands and looked at Bob.

"The man left a few things. Since you're the only family present–" he began.

"–I'm not," interjected Bob. Grub ignored him.

"–maybe you would like to take this?"

Grub reached into his pile of things and lifted up a velvety curtain of something green and lovely. It was, in fact, Bob's former coat–the very same one Fagin had laid claim to on that fateful Christmas Eve so long ago. Bob's eyes widened at the sight of it.

"It seems a shame to let such a fine coat go to waste," noted Grub.

"Thank you," said Bob, taking the garment.

"Merry Christmas, I suppose," said Grub.

Bob immediately donned the coat. Its weight felt foreign on his shoulders, but its warmth was more than welcome. He turned to take his leave.

As he moved, a fist-sized lump nudged against his chest from inside the coat. He reached a hand inside the breast pocket to find the source, but it was empty. He patted the front of the coat to confirm he hadn't imagined the lump. He hadn't. There was definitely something tucked inside the coat.

Bob reached back inside the jacket and skimmed the silky silver lining of the interior with his fingers. Soon, his fingertips came upon an unnatural seam in the fabric. Bob pried at it and discovered that a second, hidden pocket had been sewn into the silver lining of the coat. He reached inside the pocket and withdrew an enormous wad of cash.

Bob was astonished. The amount that he had lost all those years ago was there, plus a great deal more. Fagin must have sewn the pocket in after taking the coat and used it as a hiding place for all he hoarded. Now, all Bob had lost had re-emerged from the silver lining of his old trappings.

"My bonus . . ." Bob breathed aloud in a shaky, disbelieving voice. ". . . with interest."

"What?" Grub barked from behind him. Bob was turned so that the gravedigger couldn't see the trove of bills he'd just pulled from the innards of the coat.

"Just praying," Bob explained. He looked back toward the graveyard's wooden sign which bore the likeness of the Ghost of Christmas Future and whispered, "Thank you."

Bob took his leave from the cemetery. Soon, he had returned to Scrooge's place of business, coat-adorned and coal in hand.

"I got the coal," Bob announced.

Scrooge looked him over from his desk. "Is that a new coat?" he asked.

"It was a Christmas present," answered Bob.

Scrooge's eyes lit up at the word. "Ah!" he said, "Merry Christmas!"

Scrooge returned his attention to the paper on his desk, humming the tune of an upbeat Christmas carol. Bob turned towards the direction of the fireplace, intending to add his purchase of coal to the fire, then paused.

"Sir," said Bob, turning back. "You once told me you only have to buy a coat once, but you have to buy coal every time you use it. Would you prefer I save the coal?"

Scrooge looked back up at Bob with a perplexed expression. "It's Christmas, Bob," he said.

"It's the day after Christmas, sir," Bob corrected. "I can do without the coal, if you'd like."

"Nonsense!" cried Scrooge.

"It'd save the business money," offered Bob.

"What's gotten into you?" Scrooge asked.

"What's gotten into you?" Bob returned.

Scrooge smirked. "One too many Christmas spirits, I suppose."

That made Bob laugh. As he did, Scrooge joined in with a deep, bellowing laugh of his own—though Bob wasn't sure why. Then, Scrooge gestured for Bob to take a seat beside him at his desk.

Bob sat. He hadn't been here at this exact spot, he realized, since his childhood days as a young apprentice of finance beneath Scrooge and Marley. Sitting here again now, a warm feeling stirred within his chest, an echo of the unbridled gratitude that had flooded him back then.

Scrooge looked across the desk with a glimmer in his eye and began, "We were going to discuss—"

Bob found himself compelled to interrupt.

"Yes, since we were discussing the Christmas spirit, now may be a good time to ask . . . Can you help me get medicine for my son?"

It would have taken courage for Bob to ask that prior to this Christmas, but now it just felt natural.

"I know I can't control how you answer, but—" Bob was prepared to offer all sorts of justifications for his need, but Scrooge cut him off.

"Bob, I'll pay for it."

Bob looked at him with eyebrows raised. Scrooge's expression was sincere. He really meant it.

"Just like that?" asked Bob.

"Just like that."

A fit of laughter overcame Bob. When it had passed, Scrooge cleared his throat and said, "I do have one request."

"What?" asked Bob.

"Do you mind if I tell him with you?"

Bob gave him a blank look, initially confused by the request. Then he realized Scrooge was referring to Tim.

Scrooge became quiet for a moment and then explained, simply:

"I never had children of my own."

Bob understood at once.

"Of course," he told Scrooge. "We'll tell him together."

At that, a thought occurred to Bob, one which he voiced aloud.

"I have many children," he said.

"You're a very wealthy man, Bob," said Scrooge.

Bob pondered the treasure he had. He smiled.

"I am."

Scrooge smiled back.

Together, they traveled through London back towards Tim's favorite church in Camden Town. As they did, Scrooge pointed out every festive decoration with delight, tipped his hat and greeted "Merry Christmas" to every one they passed, and even dove across the street to stop the tower of parcels an old woman carried from toppling over into the snow. It was as if Bob's curmudgeon of a boss had been born anew, though in truth the change was not so jarring to Bob, who felt very much born anew himself.

Inside the church, Scrooge and Bob found Tiny Tim sitting in the front pew with his crutch beside him, head bowed and lost in prayer.

"Dear Heavenly Father," the lad whispered intently. "I pray that you watch over my father, and Mister Scrooges, and everyone we know. I pray that you heal me, and send help to . . ."

"Tim?" interrupted Bob.

Tim looked up, caught sight of Bob, and exclaimed, "Father!"

Then he saw Scrooge. His face fell.

"It's all right," explained Bob. "Mister Scrooge is here to help."

"How is your leg, Tim?" asked Scrooge.

The boy didn't answer. His bright blue eyes flitted towards his father for guidance.

Scrooge, meanwhile, looked down and leaned in slightly to look Tiny Tim in the eye.

"I know I have not been the most celebrated name in your household, but I intend to change that." He stepped closer. "Your father has told me you need medicine for your leg. I will make sure he can afford it."

Scrooge took a seat on the pew next to Tim. Tim looked back and forth between the man and his father, then let loose a laugh of mirth.

"I knew I was this way for a reason!" Tim exclaimed. He leaned in towards Scrooge and asked, "Has my condition reminded you of the one who made lame beggars walk and blind men see?"

"It helped me to learn the true spirit of Christmas," answered Scrooge.

"How do you feel, Tim?" Bob asked.

"I'm grateful," answered his son.

"Grateful?"

Tim nodded, looking towards the stained glass windows. "If I had not been a cripple, I would not have developed my spirit . . ."

"Do you think you could be grateful to have a healthy body too?" asked Bob.

Tim smiled, "I could."

"You will," assured Scrooge. "You have my whole fortune to ensure it."

"Isn't this wonderful?" exclaimed Bob, his voice echoing off the vaulted ceiling of the church. "Come. Let's go home and share the good news with your mother." He extended his arms to lift up Tim, but Tim turned away and faced forward instead.

"What are you doing?" asked Bob.

"We have to give thanks first. Giving thanks is the most important part."

He bowed his head.

"Dear holy spirits, thank you for what you have done. We are truly blessed, every one."

From somewhere outside the church, Bob could have sworn he heard a distinct, metallic clinking sound beneath the howling wind. He looked towards Scrooge for any indication that his boss had heard the sound as well. Bob saw what might have been a glint of recognition in Scrooge's eye—though perhaps he had imagined it.

"Okay, we can go now," declared Tim. Bob picked up Tiny Tim. Scrooge picked up Tim's crutch. All three of them left the church together.

As they left, they passed through the cemetery where, off in the distance, the gravedigger Gabriel Grub had been hard at work digging a new grave. Moments before, Gabriel, too, had heard an unmistakable clinking noise beneath the wind. The sound had driven him out his hole to investigate the source, to which end he had come upon a headstone labeled

MARLEY. Here, a small pile of chains and padlocks lay in the snow.

Picking them up, he called out to the figures of Scrooge, Bob, and Tim, who Grub saw were leaving the cemetery just at that moment.

"Hey!" he called to them.

Neither Bob nor Scrooge nor Tim responded to the call. Not hearing the gravedigger, they went on about their way, leaving the figure of Grub to fade away into the thick London fog.

"People always leaving things . . ." grumbled Grub.

It was evening when Bob and Tim arrived back home. The living room was empty, but a rustling sound from the kitchen told Bob where he would find his wife. He set Tim down in the living room and joined her there.

At once, Bob began rifling through the kitchen cabinets, removing old, half-drunken bottles he had stashed across the house over the years.

"What are you doing?" Emily asked.

"Emily, I have not been entirely honest with you," answered Bob as he went about his task. There was already an uncomfortable number of bottles in Bob's arms, their contents sloshing about.

"I did not speak with Scrooge yesterday," Bob went on.

"I understand," Emily said. "He can be difficult."

Bob extracted a loose brick from the kitchen's hearth, reached inside the hole, and withdrew yet another bottle.

"Do you realize," he asked Emily, "how much money I've spent on drink that should have gone to our son's care?"

"Bob, why are you telling me this?"

Bob stopped stacking bottles and looked at his wife.

"What?" he asked.

"I'm not stupid, Bob," she told him. "I know what's been going on."

Bob was taken aback. The bottles shifted in his arms so that he made a hollow, clanking sound as he turned to look at Emily full-on. "Why didn't you say anything?" he asked.

"Because I'm your wife," she replied. "I support you. Scrooge beats you down at work. You don't need that at home."

Bob looked down. "You've had every right to be upset."

"I have." They stood silent for a while. Bob set the bottles down, too ashamed to count the great many he'd retrieved from the kitchen alone. Emily broke the silence by asking, "So why are you telling me this?"

Bob looked back up at her, his expression brightening.

"Because today, I did speak with Scrooge, and we will be getting medicine for Tim within the week."

Emily's jaw dropped.

"Really?"

"It's all paid for."

At once, Bob saw tears welling up in Emily's eyes. He crossed the kitchen and put his arms around her.

"Does Tim know?" she asked.

"He does," said Bob.

Tim's voice piped up from the living room, charged to the brim with childish excitement.

"Mister Scrooge visited us at church. I prayed for him, and now he has the Christmas spirit."

Emily laughed.

"Emily," Bob whispered in her ear as they embraced, "you've always supported me. Can you support me in a different way?"

"Of course."

Together, they went through the house and raided every nook and cranny to retrieve every bottle Bob had ever stashed. They put what they found in a large bag, which Bob promptly handed over to Emily.

"Don't let me see where you get rid of this," he instructed her. She nodded and left with the bag. Bob closed the door behind her and awaited her return, knowing she left with the last drink he'd ever have.

Tiny Tim hobbled over on his crutch. He gave Bob a hug.

"Thank you for taking care of me," he said. Bob nodded.

The next day, Bob and Emily took Tim to a doctor. His examination complete, the physician was now scribbling something on a scrap of paper as he spoke his diagnosis aloud.

"Your son is missing something in his diet. Very common." The doctor explained how sailors had learned that a deficiency of certain foods caused scurvy and other illnesses. Tim was likely suffering from a similar malnutrition. He ripped the sheet he'd been writing on off the pad and handed it to Bob. "Give him limes and castor oil, and he'll gradually make a full recovery."

Bob took the sheet. He looked at Tim and saw what could only be the mirror of his own expression in his son's young face—a perfect portrait of relief. Tim was going to be okay.

The weeks passed, and a different version of the future than the one Bob had been shown in his visions began to take shape. He noticed it one day when he found himself in his best suit stepping into Scrooge's place of business. Bob had just returned from the London Stock Exchange, where their new investments had blossomed into unforeseen profits for the business. He passed a large envelope of money to his boss. Scrooge took the envelope, counted its contents, and passed back a generous portion of the earnings to Bob. Bob took these back to his office, where the two portly gentlemen were awaiting his arrival. They graciously accepted the money as a donation and took their leave. Bob marveled at the fact that not only was Scrooge now a man who gave, but that they had so much to give, and he was even as grateful for the money that left his hands as the money that was placed in them.

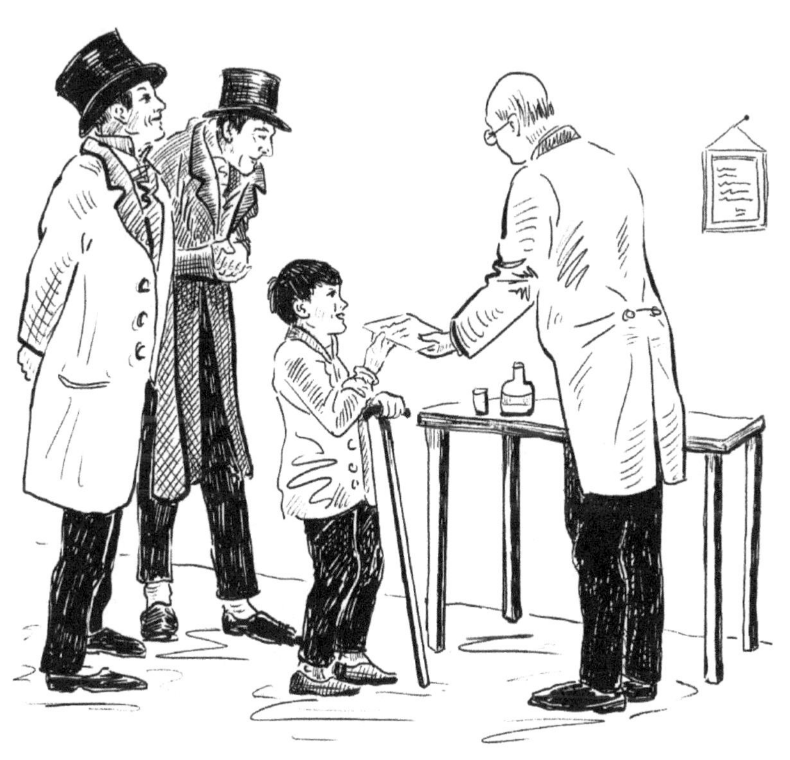

On Bob's desk sat a large crate of limes and a few small bottles of castor oil, the most recent shipment in a regular line of supply Bob and Scrooge had arranged. Limes were not natural to England. Even their presence here was a miracle, albeit a miracle of industry.

One miracle begat another. When the day was over, Bob would take those foods back home to Tiny Tim who, thanks to his newfound diet, was making a full recovery. He had already grown so strong and healthy that Bob could scarcely believe it. Soon, he would be walking on his own without the need for a crutch of any kind.

The months passed. One clear spring day, Bob arrived at Scrooge's establishment to find the sign that had always marked his workplace SCROOGE AND MARLEY to be missing. In its place was a new sign, one that read SCROOGE AND CRATCHIT.

Bob was nearly moved to tears at the first sight of the sign. It was, in fact, the latest in a long string of "merry surprises" which Scrooge had taken to bestowing on friend and stranger alike ever since that Christmas.

More months passed, and soon Christmas time arrived again. That Christmas Eve, the Cratchit family found themselves gathered around the dinner table with three new additions since last year: the two portly gentlemen and Scrooge. Atop the table–steaming, filling the room with its savory aroma–there lay a Christmas goose far bigger than any they'd ever seen before.

Scrooge offered a toast.

"A toast to the founder of the feast, Mister Bob Cratchit!"

Everyone raised their cups. Some of them were raising wine, others warm cider. Bob was raising simple water. He'd had his fill of Spirits and wanted nothing more than to be where he was. Cup lifted high, he looked around the room at his friends and family.

"No amount of gratitude is too great," he said, "for what we have been given in the Christmas spirit."

At this, Tiny Tim leapt up to stand on his chair with both feet sturdy and firm, no crutch in sight.

"And God bless us, every one!"

AFTERWORD

BY DAVID JOHN MAROTTA

Why couldn't Bob Cratchit live off his salary?

This was the question I had when reflecting on Charles Dickens's *A Christmas Carol.* He made enough money despite his large family. Large families were normal in that period, and he earned as much as a constable. Where did all his money go?

As a financial planner, I've learned that income is rarely the problem. Whatever your income is, I have probably met a family of four living off half your salary. And I probably know a couple of families who make twice what you make and can't seem to save anything. My own lifestyle, like Warren Buffet's, is very frugal. And as a rule, my wealthy clients are my most frugal clients. Wealth is what you save and invest—not what you spend. You can live rich or you can be rich.

One couple came to me for financial advice. They had inherited over a million dollars. They had put a down payment on an expensive house. They joined the local country club. They had purchased all the latest technology. They spent more on new shoes, clothes, and accessories in a year than I probably had in the past decade. And they were running out of money.

As schoolteachers, their salaries were both very modest. And the windfall gain that they had received quickly destroyed their finances because of their new lavish lifestyle. It was unsustainable. They could not even afford to maintain the mortgage payments.

It may seem insignificant, but the difference between saving a million dollars and not saving anything is about ten dollars a day.

So, looking at Bob Cratchit's budget would be the first course of action to see why Bob couldn't live on a salary that half of London could only dream about.

And that was when I realized that Bob's financial personality type was that of a spendthrift, the opposite financial personality type of Scrooge. Bob is both fearful of and careless with his money.

In 2005, I wrote the Christmas article, "Why is Bob Cratchit So Poor?" explaining Bob's financial personality. Here is a sample of my description:

"Spendthrifts are some of the most pleasant people to be around. They are socially outgoing and often demonstrate their own friendliness by buying things for other people.

"As a typical spendthrift, Bob was probably raised in poverty. Buying gives spendthrifts great pleasure in life.

Spending produces an addictive high and helps them establish their social status. In Bob's mind, raising his social status mistakenly depends on the amount he spends—not the amount he saves.

"For Bob Cratchit, living within a budget and saving money would be like setting out to deprive yourself and suffer. Spendthrifts live for the pleasure of the moment. Eating out or buying clothes are viewed as immediate pleasures for relatively small amounts of money. They do not realize that the purpose of budgeting and saving is to make sure they are spending money on the things they really want instead of frittering it away.

"On Christmas Eve, Mr. Scrooge brings his banker's book home with him to review all evening. Spendthrifts, on the other hand, almost never keep any records of their purchases. But records would show the Cratchit family that Bob's spending habits are exposing his family to want and suffering.

"Christmas grew in popularity during the Victorian era as a time of feasting and a time for those of stature to show their affluence. During the Victorian era, Christmas was more about food than about giving gifts, and the Cratchit family is determined to show that they know how to keep Christmas.

"The Cratchits buy a beautiful goose and then admire it for its cheapness. Spendthrifts typically go bankrupt saving money. We are not told what Bob paid for his Christmas goose, but stories of the day suggest that a goose conservatively cost about 400 pence (1.5 pounds). At this amount, the Cratchit family goose is costing the family a year's supply of medical attention for the entire family.

"Many spendthrifts justify their purchases as 'investments.' They often buy jewelry, clothes, or even fancy houseware as an investment to provide themselves an excuse to gain the trappings of a richer lifestyle. This purposeful self-deception shows the depth of a typical spendthrift's denial. An investment is something which pays you money, not an article of clothing.

"But the Cratchit family exhibits typical spendthrift behavior when it comes to clothing. On Christmas day, Bob Cratchit confers on his son Peter a shirt in honor of his apprenticeship. It was common in the day for the rich to go through the Parks to show off their finery. And Peter is amazed to find himself so gallantly attired that he too is anxious to show off his fashionable new linen in the park.

"Even Mrs. Cratchit is described as 'brave in ribbons, which are cheap and make a goodly show for sixpence.' Making a good show is important for spendthrifts. Mrs. Cratchit's ribbons cost about two to three weeks of medical attention for the entire family. Their second daughter, Belinda, is also brave in ribbons–another three weeks of medical attention.

"The Cratchit family is clearly living beyond their means."

Chronicling Bob Cratchit's overspending is not difficult. If you read the original story looking for overspending, there are many examples, each less important than saving your son's life.

In my article, I left out much of the overspending that I found. The Cratchits have apples and oranges on their table. Oranges in the middle of winter were a costly expense. He purchased lemons for his gin. Since Tiny Tim might have been suffering from a vitamin deficiency, giving those lemons to Tiny Tim might have cured his ailment!

But one of the primary criticisms I left out was how much Bob spent on alcohol. I stopped short of saying that Bob had a drinking problem, but he did. The word alcoholism wasn't invented until later, but Charles Dickens himself was something of an alcoholic. Dickens preached moderation but practiced drinking heavily. At the end of his life, he was living off not much more than booze and raw eggs.

Given the terrible quality of the water in London at the time, alcoholic drinks were probably much better than water from the Thames. Nevertheless, Bob Cratchit, like Dickens, seems to enjoy his booze a little too much.

When the Ghost of Christmas Present brings Scrooge to the Cratchit residence, we find Bob compounding "some hot mixture in a jug with gin and lemons" stirring it round and round and putting it on the hob to simmer. Later, that same jug goes round and round the family. Bob applies "half-a-quartern of ignited brandy" to Mrs. Cratchit's pudding.

There was sufficient alcohol consumed for Bob to blame his being late for work the next day on the fact that he was "making rather merry yesterday."

In addition to giving him a raise and helping his family, one of the reformed Scrooge's gifts to Bob is to share a "Christmas bowl of smoking bishop," a spiced wine made from port, red wine, Seville oranges, sugar, and cloves. This must have been a great treat to the gin-drinking Bob. Dickens even makes an alcohol pun at the end of the story writing, "He had no further intercourse with Spirits, but lived upon the Total Abstinence Principle."

As such, it was not a difficult switch to focus on Bob's drink instead of Scrooge's thrift.

In the original story, the Cratchit family seem to despise Scrooge. He is "the Ogre of the family." The mention of his name casts a dark shadow on their celebration. Mrs. Cratchit describes him as "an odious, stingy, hard, unfeeling man."

Such a description always struck me as unwarranted simply by what we are told in the original text. Many employers of the day were much harder on their employees than we see in Scrooge's actions. And the question of how Mrs. Cratchit would even have such an opinion of Mr. Scrooge always bothered me. Her impressions of Scrooge must have been conveyed from what Bob communicated to his wife. Yet Bob is the one trying to defend Mr. Scrooge while his wife is attacking him, and her attacks are probably based on nothing other than what Bob has told her.

That oddity got me thinking that perhaps what Bob communicated to his wife about Mr. Scrooge was not fair to Mr. Scrooge. Bob knows the information wasn't accurate, but he can't admit lying to his wife and therefore he defends Mr. Scrooge.

What lie would cause Mrs. Cratchit's invectives? Obviously something about money not being paid when it should have been paid. But in the opening of the story, Scrooge is described as punctually paying everything he should.

Mrs. Cratchit is too upset with Scrooge to think that all Scrooge did was not pay enough. He is paying generously for Bob's work. It seems as though Mrs. Cratchit believes

Scrooge has been stingy with what was owed or at least with what was promised. Yet Bob defends Scrooge.

From that anomaly, I devised that Bob had been paid a sum of money, had lost it, and from embarrassment had not told his wife the truth. Bob being paid and still not having enough could also be one of the causes for the falling out of his relationship with Scrooge. Scrooge would view it as very careless accounting to squander a bonus or raise and seem to have less money than before the windfall.

This gave me the set up for the story. What about the end? How does Bob Cratchit need to change and grow in order to receive Scrooge's gift at the end of the original story?

Although Scrooge is the only one who has saved enough to right the situation, unless Bob also changes, his spendthrift ways will be difficult to overcome. Only Bob's change of heart will help keep his family out of debt such that Scrooge's kindness will have an effect. Bob has to be ready to accept Scrooge's kindness. Thus, *The Haunting of Bob Cratchit* was conceived.

Originally, I wrote several articles on a Christmas Carol at "Marotta On Money," our corporate website. I wrote one article each year for several years. Those articles dealt with the financial personalities according to Bert Whitehead, another financial advisor, in his book *Facing Financial Dysfunction.*

It turns out that every character in the story has a different financial personality. And there is much to be learned from their attitudes toward money. Bob was the second article to be written. The investigation of those articles eventually led to this book. Many of the details of this novel, like the cure for Tiny Tim's illness or Bob getting a deal on a Christmas goose due to the amount he spends on alcohol, come from historical research. My exploration of these characters is based in the original text of Charles Dickens's *A Christmas Carol.*

You can read those original articles, learn about our process, and discover more about the world of this book and Charles Dickens's *A Christmas Carol* at:

https://www.marottaonmoney.com/haunting-afterword

www.ingramcontent.com/pod-product-compliance
Lightning Source LLC
Chambersburg PA
CBHW060538310726
48982CB00009B/1298/J

9781736272305